Basics of Life

12 Short Stories

Edited by Steve Rossiter

A project of The Australian Literature Review

ISBN-13: 978-0-9871242-1-0

DEDICATION

This book is dedicated to storytellers; those who create original fictional scenarios to entertain, intrigue, inspire and provide a catalyst for independent thought.

Basics of Life was compiled from short story submissions to The Australian Literature Review website (www.auslit.net). It features the work of mostly emerging fiction writers, with a few established writers in the mix.

CONTENTS

SURVIVAL

1

DO OR DIE

BY DEREK TAYLOR

As the hot metal meets my skin, flashes of a metal playground slide from my childhood enter my mind. In the midday sun the slide could get hot enough to feel as though it was burning bare skin on contact. Some of the kids in town wouldn't use the slide on a sunny day but I couldn't resist. It was alright as long as only the clothed parts of my body touched the metal. Sometimes other kids would watch on and cringe or howl with laughter if my shirt rode up or I put out an arm to steady myself and got a dose of hot metal.

I've been falling down life's slide in my underwear for the past three years and people are cringing and laughing from the sidelines. In that sense, it's ironic that reaching the bottom of the slide brings me to more hot metal. I had fired a round into a tree to see what

7

damage it would do and the barrel is still hot. The heat spreads through my temple.

As I think over my choice, the heat dissipates and I lower the gun.

If I pull the trigger nothing will survive; at least nothing I would be proud to have survive. I appreciate the irony of wanting something to be proud of when I won't be around to feel that pride. I appreciate the irony of wanting something to carry on after I cut my life short by choice. At 25, and living my life as I have, I can hardly claim to be going out on a high note after a lifetime of achievement.

I don't believe I'll look on from an afterlife and follow the results of my work. Then why have I not ended my sorry little life? I have come up with an answer of sorts. I'll leave you to judge if it is a good one.

I try to imagine what it would be like to be dead. I picture blackness; silence; a void. Then I reason that I would not experience this but instead there would be no me to experience even a void. I keep trying to reconcile an idea of what death will be like with an answer which seems to be that I will *no longer exist*.

All I know is that, right now, ceasing to exist holds more terror than any suffering life can throw at me.

What happens next is a muddle. I hear sirens. I see the red and blue lights. There's a young woman. There's yelling. There's running. I'm not a wanted criminal, but I don't have a good explanation for the gun and the shot.

I take the woman back to my place.

She slumps in the chair and asks, 'If you want to die, why aren't you dead?'

'That's a rude question,' I respond.

How much have I told her? How long did it take to get back here?

'I'm sorry. Maybe I should do something polite and kidnap someone at gunpoint!'

If she's talking to me like this, maybe I've been too soft on her - given the circumstances. But I'd like to think I'm not a bad guy.

'What's your name?'

'My name is none of your business.'

'If we're going to get along-'

'I'll stop you there.'

I take a breath. 'I'm the one with the gun. You're in

this situation. Yes, it's my fault. But that's where we're at, so let's try to make this as pleasant as we can.'

'You know what'd be pleasant?' She folds her arms and awaits my reply.

I humour her. 'What?'

'If you *let me go*. That'd be *really* pleasant.'

'It's not going to happen. Not yet. So drop it.'

'Then when?'

'I don't know.'

'So what now?'

'Can you tell me again what we're doing?'

'We're going to my childhood home town,' I explain, 'to destroy a slide in a children's playground.'

'...because the metal felt hot when you touched it 15 years ago?'

'Because I'm sliding into oblivion.'

She gives me the stink eye. 'You have a *delusion* about a slide so you're going to take away the fun of a town full of children?'

I open my mouth to rebut but I have no rebuttle. 'Yes.'

'That's healthy,' she mutters under her breath.

'Wow. The infamous slide. And here I was expecting it to be adorned with fire-breathing goblins.'

10

She feigns an inspection of the slide. 'Nope, just a normal slide which provides dozens of kids with enjoyment each day.'

I look the slide up and down then scratch my head.

'You have no idea how you're going to destroy the slide, do you?'

'I've got ideas,' I assert.

'Let's hear them.'

'Quiet. I'm thinking.'

'We came all this way and you've got nothing.' She throws her hands up in amazement. 'Unbelievable!'

'What if we get sledgehammers and bang it up so bad they have to remove it?' I suggest.

'The slide is your nemesis and that's the best you've got?' She looks disappointed. 'How does someone even turn a slide into their nemesis? That's messed up.'

'That's not helping. You know,' I say, raising an eyebrow, 'You've got plausible deniability here. If you get caught, you can say I made you do it. Haven't you ever wanted to break something with no consequences?'

It's like a switch flips in her head. 'Circular saws.' There is a mad glint in her eye. 'Cutting torches. We can steal them from the metalwork room at the high school. The gas tanks are heavy but we could get them into the car.'

What have I done? Have I corrupted her? ... Or is she about to corrupt me?

'Those ideas are good too. What else can we think of?'

'This is the one,' I say, taking two of the cheapest saws off the shelf at the hardware shop.

'I still think cutting torches would be cooler.'

'But saws will be easier. Now we just need one of those power point things that plugs into the car's cigarette lighter,'

She scoffs.

'Let's hear it.'

'You want to power not one but two saws from the car's cigarette lighter?' She scoffs again.

'I used to know someone who ran a vacuum cleaner from his.'

'Have you known anyone who ran a power tool from it?'

'It will work.'

'It's not working,' she hisses. We have agreed to whisper but 'whispering' from the bottom of the hill to the top over the sound of a saw defeats the purpose.

'Maybe the extension cord is losing power before it gets to you,' I hiss back.

12

'Then is yours working?'

Mine is not so much cutting through the metal as it is scratching it. 'Not as fast as I'd hoped.'

'I told you.'

I unplug the extension cord, hoping my saw will work better with all the power going to it. I don't detect any improvement.

I look at her as she waits expectantly. 'This is not working.'

'I can't believe I let you talk me into this,' I say, parked by the high school metalwork room.

She shoots me a glance that says 'just get on with it.'

I begin lining the back of the car up with the metalwork room's glass double doors which swing open in the middle.

'Wait. What are you doing?' she protests.

'What? I'm ramming the door.'

Her eyes say 'are you insane?' She reaches around to the floor behind her seat and retrieves the tyre iron. She gets out of the car, pulls her jumper over her head and wraps it around an end of the tyre iron.

Smart. That'll make a lot less noise.

With a quick thrust, she pops a hole in the top-left corner of the glass pane in the bottom half of the right

13

door. She slips her hand in, unlocks the doors and opens them wide. She raises a hand, signalling for me to wait, then dashes inside.

What now?

For a second I wonder if she's made a run for it and the business with the doors has just been a distraction. Then she returns with broom in hand, sweeps the broken glass against the wall and waves me in.

For the first time since all this began, she doesn't look combative. Dare I say it? She even looks friendly.

I back in and by the time I'm out of the car door she's lighting one of the cutting torches.

I open my mouth, but before I can get a word out she directs the torch to illuminate a padlocked metal latch on a frame holding the cutting torch's gas bottle in place.

She zaps the latch for a few seconds and finishes the job with the tyre iron.

I open the car's back hatch and toss in a protective face mask for use with the cutting torch. We ease the gas bottle against the back of the car then lift the heavy base and push it in. As we're pushing, our forearms touch and I'm surprised by the softness of her skin in contrast to the firmness of her muscles pushing against the weight of the gas bottle.

With the bottle in, my eyes wander to her forearm.

14

I've just felt and up to her bare shoulder, exposed by her tank top, rising and falling slightly from the exertion.

Uh oh, she's looking me in the eyes.

'What's wrong? Never touched a woman's arm before?' she asks, but without her usual bite behind it. 'Come on. Let's go.'

As we drive into the playground the headlights reflect off the slide's shiny metal sides.

We maneuver the gas bottle into place midway down the slide. She returns to the top to stand lookout and I slip the protective mask on.

The torch showers sparks as it contacts the metal and eats it away.

I can't describe the feeling of finally having my moment of victory over something which has been eating at *me* for so long and so deeply. If I had to describe it, I'd say I feel... empty.

Is this my life's purpose? To destroy a piece of playground equipment because I've somehow contorted it into a symbol of my descent through life? Where to next? How do I get through another 60 or 70 years?

Pulling the torch away, I lift the face mask to get a better look at the damage.

A distinct little scar is sunken into the lip of the slide.

I look to her for... something; maybe reassurance that I don't have to do this and that I can go home.

She's too far away to register that anything more than time-wasting is going on. She taps her wrist to indicate I should hurry.

But there's a problem. I can't go home and forget all this ever happened. I don't have anywhere I feel at home; just temporary and inadequate refuges from life.

The thing is I can't run away from life. It's always there, waiting to be filled. Until I die.

With the thought of death, flashes of falling down life's hot slide - this slide - enter my mind and I strike out with the cutting torch. As I carve through the metal, I'm merely going through the motions. Nothing is getting better.

I watch her and think of what could be. But it could never be. I'd drag her down that slide with me, and we'd fall out half way down. That wouldn't be fair on her. I know what I have to do.

I heard somewhere that the day you die plays on loop in your spirit's mind forever. I never believed it, but I hope it's somehow true, because I've felt something today. I've had some level of connection with another human being. I've come to the conclusion that living is a more terrifying prospect for me than dying. Life holds the responsibility not to cause hurt to others, whereas death does not carry that burden. That gives me peace. There is no battle inside. A burden has been lifted. In some sad and strange way, tonight has been the best night of my life.

2

TWENTY DAYS

BY SOPHIE MASSON

Eighteen--nineteen--twenty red crosses on the calendar; how many more would there have to be? Twenty days since Michael had left with the sheep and his offsider Craig; twenty days since Gillian and the child had stood at the gate and waved them off; twenty days since, no longer able to see even the most remote cloud of dust churned up by the heavy wheels of the truck and the trailer for the bikes, Gillian had turned to the child and said, with a determined attempt at levity, 'Well, then, we two will have to entertain each other till Daddy gets back, won't we!' Twenty days since the child had given her back look for look, and nodded, silently, challengingly. Twenty days. Twenty long, long days.

Practically all the neighbours' sheep had already gone south to greener pastures by the time Michael decided he could not wait for a rain-miracle any longer. There must be a great gathering of stockmen and their mobs out there in the stock routes and reserves, Gillian thought; quite some party it must be, all those sheep out on the road, and motorists cursing as yet another mob drifted and jostled across the tar. Michael had wanted to there with the sheep for a fair while now; he had left it as long as he possibly could, for pregnant Gillian's sake. But it was she who had said to him, one morning, 'Please, darling, take them out on the road, I don't think I can bear it any longer..'

She meant, I can't bear listening to the sheep bleating, their pathetic rushing for the last bit of hay thrown out from the ute, your worried face, drawing down into the same harsh lines as the steadily skeletonising landscape under the merciless, beautiful blue sky.

When she'd first come here, two years ago--could it really be only that long ago?--the whole place was a mass of knee-deep pale green and yellow grass, thick, waving in all directions like an endless, shimmering sea

19

to the very edges of the horizon. On the edges of the horizon, the earth curved, noticeably, enclosing the farm, and it was as if this place was all the world there was. Sometimes, you could see cars or trucks moving along the road on the horizon's outer edge, and in the pure, refracting light, it was as though they were ships, perhaps those of the Argonauts seeking the Golden Fleece, sailing the limits of the known sea. She watched them as if she were a remote goddess watching the far-off strange commerce of human beings; their bustling meaningless busyness.

The farm had been named Grasmere, by Michael's great grandparents, who'd come out from the Lake District in Britain, but the sign writer had never heard of that far away place and assumed it to be 'Grass Mere', taking it to be a some kind of daft joke on the farm's most dominant feature: mere grass perhaps? There were a few short wilga trees dotted here and there in the paddocks, and rich deep brown soil, and thousands of little native flowers in amongst the lush mixed native and exotic grasses. The kangaroos and emus that jostled the sheep for a living in this rich land were not too much resented in times of plenty; and the land's fragility was not apparent, at least not to Gillian.

20

Born and bred in the city, and used to hills and plunging bays and steep slopes, the flat grassland had charmed and delighted her. Its strange, deceptive horizons and enormous skies and secretive animal pathways in among the prairie grasses seemed to promise endless freedom, recalled to her mind childhood dreamings of nomadic horsemen ranging over immense steppes, and herself as a Scythian princess in armour, carrying a bow, the equal of her brothers and father. She had pestered her parents to let her learn to ride, back in the city, and to everyone's surprise but her own, had done rather well at it. When she married Michael, she had assumed that at last she'd have a horse of her own and go out on musters and long droves. But here, in sheep country, few people used horses any more; it was all motorbikes, two wheelers and three wheelers and four-wheelers, and she hated them with a passion that Michael found amusing.

'You needed to marry a cattleman if you wanted horses, love,' he'd say, smiling at her when she complained how the bikes stank of oil and grease and hot metal, all the industrial smells she hated and thought she'd put behind her when she came to live in the country. She gave up on the idea of horses, but refused to ride a bike, and instead walked out to the sheepyards to help with dipping, or bumped along in

21

the ute to the far paddocks to help dose the young ewes
with flystrike powder, or go round the lambing ewes to
check all was well. She went on long walks too and
sketched and sketched. She was still selling her
drawings and paintings to her agent in the city, though
he was complaining that her work was getting more and
more realistic, that she didn't have the fantasy edge
anymore that she used to have. Soon, she thought, he'll
tell me not to bother. Yet, the first year, she'd painted
possibly the best thing she'd ever done, a massive
picture, fantastically detailed, like a three-dimensional
map, really, of the farm as a kind of fantasy realm, the
Mere of Grass, with every paddock name--Long Mile,
Shortfall, Wilga, and so on--functioning as the name of
a village, or manor, whatever. At the edge of the Mere
of Grass, there was an inner sea, with a black-sailed
ship and a white-sailed ship sailing towards the far
horizon and the outer sea, where, just as in medieval
maps, dragons and sea serpents writhed and waited. In
the centre of the picture, where the house stood in
mundanity, there was a castle, with flying turrets and
drawbridge; and she'd drawn two tiny figures, a blond-
haired man and a dark-eyed woman, standing at the
door in welcome, hands outstretched. She had intended
selling the picture, but somehow could not bear to part
with it, though she knew her agent would have raved

over it. It stayed there on the wall of the room Michael called her studio but which more and more in recent times had become the child's bolthole.

The child... no, not the child wriggling and diving in Gillian's distended belly, but Michael's daughter by his first marriage, living with them since only a few months ago, because of the death of her mother in a road accident. Gillian had been more than ready to welcome the child, horrified by the trauma the poor little thing must have suffered, full of a certain expectation that she would soon grow to love Michael's child, no matter what. And Michael had assured her Bianca was just like her--bookish, clever, prone to dreaming and imagination. It would be easy for them to get on, she'd thought. But alas, Michael's child--the child Bianca, flaxen-haired and blue-eyed and graceful as some orphaned mite in a fairytale--did not respond to Gillian's advances and did not seem interested in anything at all. At least not anything that Gillian wanted to do, or suggested, or spoke about. She spent the days and hours when she was not at school, or rattling along in the school bus, aimlessly wandering about in the top paddock, near the gate, or reading, or playing the rather dull computer games Michael had installed for her on his office machine. She changed as soon as she heard her father's step in the hall, as soon as she heard the

23

sound of his ute drawing up in the dust of the drive. Then she would be bright, lively, chattering, when only a couple of minutes before, in Gillian's company, she had been silent, uncommunicative--not sullen, exactly, just blank, as if Gillian were not human, but, say, a tree, or worse, a wall, or a table: something that you could not expect to interact with at all. At first, Gillian had taken little notice, telling herself that poor little Bianca was bound to feel some very complicated emotions indeed; her mother had not taken at all well to Michael's remarrying, though it had been her who had left him, and no doubt the child had heard all kinds of things about her. She was patient and kind and gentle with Bianca, and never told Michael that there was anything wrong, and so of course he saw nothing wrong. For when Bianca was around him, it was as if she were a different person; and even Gillian was included then in her reflected glory.

The only thing of Gillian's that Bianca was remotely interested in was the picture in the studio, the fantasy-map of the farm. She spent hours just looking at it, and Gillian had found her once with her nose pressed up close against it, as if she were physically trying to get into the picture. She was murmuring something as she did so, jerky little words that seemed to be in no language Gillian had ever heard. That did not concern

24

her; as a child, she too, had made up all kinds of 'languages'; as a Tolkien-worshipping adolescent, she'd started writing some down and devising grammars for them, but gave up soon enough, bored by linguistic formulae that seemed altogether too close to mathematics for her liking. But Bianca had started when she'd become aware that Gillian was in the room too; a strange look had come into her eyes, a look that even now Gillian could not interpret properly.

Perhaps it was from then that Gillian's feelings towards Bianca began to change. Or perhaps it was as her pregnancy advanced. She began to feel there was something of a calculated malice in the child's rejection of her, and a superstitious dread fell on her whenever Bianca's eyes fell on her own round belly. In his innocence, Michael assumed that Bianca was as thrilled as he was by the coming arrival of a new brother or sister; Gillian thought she knew better. The child's blue eyes, it seemed to her, were as mercilessly, blankly hostile as the drought-sky; her slender, pale little hands seemed to become claw-like at any mention of the new baby. The child hated her, she thought, breathlessly; hated her and the new life growing inside her, and the hatred was growing, becoming a thing that could literally endanger Gillian and her child..

25

Stop it, she would tell herself sternly. You are just falling into the archetypal wicked stepmother trap. Bianca's just a child; you're an adult. She's lost her mother, trying to share her father; of course she hates you, or thinks she does. When the baby's born, everything will change. You'll see. We'll be one happy family. But who knows if all those wicked stepmothers, the ones that wanted to poison and kill and destroy their stepchildren, what if it was just a matter of survival, a fight to the death? What if the children really, really hated them and just wanted to destroy everything between their father and this usurping new woman? What if children, especially daughters, have a much greater power than people will admit? Oh. Stop it. Stop it.

Michael noticed something was wrong between them; you'd have had to blind and deaf not to. But either he didn't want to, or couldn't, imagine the depth of antipathy that existed between his daughter and his wife. But the obscure unease that was obviously in him kept him at the farm for much longer than he should have stayed, for the sheep's sake, and that was highly unusual, for Michael was a born sheepman, and loved his charges, though he would never have admitted to it. But he was relieved when Gillian told him he must go, for he knew it was crunch time for the sheep if he'd stayed even a day longer. He must have thought, too, that if she urged him to go, then things must be alright. Indeed, Gillian managed to persuade him that this would be a 'good opportunity' for herself and Bianca to 'get to know each other better'. She did not try to persuade him to take her with him, for that would have meant taking Bianca too, anyway; and though she knew that some women went on droving camps these days, she honestly did not fancy it. At least, not tagging along, with Bianca, and the stockman Craig. Alone with Michael, that would have been different. At least for a while. She knew enough about farming life by now to know that if you did not have an instinctive feel for land and animals and things agricultural in general, you could soon become very bored indeed, when there were not even other things to distract you, just keeping an eye on sheep grazing on the roadside. No; she would be fine here, she assured Michael; she'd do lots of sketching; though it was school holidays, she'd try and do things with Bianca, take her to the cinema in the town an hour and a half away, organise school friends to come and play or sleepover with the child, whatever. They'd find lots to do. Won't we, Bianca? she had appealed to the child, who, because her father was there, anxiously awaiting her confirmation, smiled in a regal way.

But now, it was twenty days since he'd gone. At least fifteen since Gillian had run out of ideas and patience with the child. At least six since she'd begun to lose hope that it would start to rain, and Michael would return soon. Two days since he'd last rung. He'd taken the mobile phone with him, but it did not always work, out on the road, and he wasn't always close by a public phone to ring her every day. He'd promised to ring at least every three days and had more than fulfilled that promise. She clung to the idea that she'd hear his voice soon; because he was a reminder that there was another world, beyond the house, the garden, the paddocks that stretched dry and flat and dead in every direction, and the endless, merciless sky.

For Bianca refused to leave the farm. In the last three or four days, she had point-blank refused to come on any shopping expedition or to visit any friends; she hung out in the top paddock, by the gate, waiting by the big wilga tree for hours on end, so that Gillian was forced to trudge out to her every so often to check she was OK and to bring her little snacks and drinks, things that Bianca accepted without comment, as her due, but without apparent hostility, either. Once, she had even unbent so far as to say to her stepmother, 'I saw the ships again today… they're closer, now… they're coming to help me..' but clammed up when Gillian tried

28

to reply in kind, about how she'd seen them too, one with white sails, one with black, which was why she'd put them on her picture. The funny thing was that though it was deeply annoying, it also made Gillian feel a little more sympathetic towards the child again, to make her remember that it was a child she was dealing with, and not a fledgling witch.

Twenty days… Gillian put down the red pen with which she'd marked the calendar, and sighed deeply. She'd listened to the weather report last night, and heard the weatherman claiming that a big low was on its way. But she'd heard those things before; big lows which blew up over the ocean, steamed in over the coast, hit the dividing range with a big splat and evaporated over the western plains. To see distant clouds and know that somewhere, somewhere that didn't need it, it was raining fit to burst dams and flood already sodden paddocks, was to add insult to injury. She'd thought of doing a rain dance, but knew no steps, no words.

Now, she got up, and driven by some aimless impulse, came into her studio and stood in front of her painting, staring absently at it for the first time in many weeks. A funny twisted gaiety rose in her. She was the queen of this painted place, the chatelaine, the Morgana le Fay of this particular Avalon. She could do anything in this realm. Perhaps she should take up her brush, paint in a big low or something, skimming lightly in on big gusty gales and driving rain, saturating the entire realm? Why not?

She picked up a brush, and stood back to look carefully at how she would do it. Then she gave an exclamation, so sharp that it actually felt to her like a physical pain. For the tiny figures in the castle door-- they were no longer a man and woman, but a man... and a child. A child with flaxen hair, confident, relaxed, the man's hand on her shoulder. Of the woman, there was no sign... not a trace... except yes... there, in the barred window at the bottom, the dungeon window, there was a face, a woman's face, staring hopelessly, the dark eyes sunken. And under the window, in the soil just below, a tiny cross...

Some deep detached part of Gillian stood and gazed in admiration, knowing that the hand that had made these changes was an artist's hand; a little awkward, perhaps, a little immature, but remarkably vivid, for all that, quick, almost cruel brushstrokes giving somehow an unforgettable picture of calm triumph on the one hand and wild desperation on the

30

other. Yet the greater part of Gillian rose up in horror and revolt at what she was seeing. Her breath whistled in her throat, burnt in her chest. The child's malice seemed truly without bounds…

Without stopping to think, she flung out of the house, and instead of walking, started up the ute, throwing it into gear with such force that it kangaroo-hopped down the drive for an instant. Bianca heard the roar of the engine; Gillian saw her raise her head. But then she turned away, again, indifferent, and somehow it was that turning away, as if nothing her stepmother could do would ever be of any interest or connection or anxiety to her, that filled Gillian with a terrifying fury. She threw the vehicle up the road, straight towards the slight figure waiting at the gate, her mind and heart roaring with fire, her veins full of what seemed like the most virulent poison in the world, corrosive and powerful and deadly as dragon's blood.

At the last moment, the child looked up and saw her. Saw her face, her real face, not the kind-but-irritating-stepmother-who-understands-and-tries, but the wild and wicked witch, the poisoner, the killer, the she-dragon, fiercer by far than the male, bearing down, unstoppable and inconsolable. Bianca gave a shriek; threw herself sideways in a desperate attempt to get

31

away; tripped over a wilga root; went sprawling, flung her arms up over her head, and fell, and was still. But there was the sound of breaking glass, and the roar of waves, and Gillian, braking so hard that the tyres smelt burnt, and the car spinning, sliding, the steering wheel in her hands like a loose, crazed, determined thing, the horizon whirling, throwing her to the limits, the limits of everything, of love, of truth, of life itself. She saw the ship, then, tacking swiftly towards her, flying black sails, for mourning, for sorrow, for endless night, coming not to help her, but to avenge, to destroy… She saw the captain, standing on the deck, fierce dark face alight with savage glee, knowing that the castle would be sacked, the crops burnt, the land put to the torch, everyone and everything slaughtered as the brass-faced goddess of war and destruction rampaged over all. She heard the bang as the world ended; and then silence.

Nothing to be seen, from the one barred window, but endless harsh blue sky, stretching on and on and on. Nothing to be heard, in this dungeon deep below the castle, but endless, thick silence. The prisoner groaned, and stumbled back to her pallet, her head in her hands.

This was her last morning on earth. Last night had

been her own last night. And she'd not rested, but had the dream again, the tormenting dream of another life, a life strange in its details, yet close to her own heart-knowledge. For there was a child in that dream, too, a child just like her own stepdaughter Blanche. But in the dream, the child was called Bianca; and her own dream-self was called Gillian, and not Julian. Only Michael had the same name. And that was perhaps the hardest thing of all..

The door rattled. She heard a key turn in the rusty lock. Her flesh crept. They had come. There was nothing left for her now. She could not even die with honour, for she must expiate her crime, the crime of attempting to murder her own husband's daughter, while the girl's father was away. It was Michael, Prince Michael of the Mere of Grass, admiral of the fleet and lord justice of the court, who had judged her, condemned her, and would now wait, black-robed, straight-backed, stony-faced and hollow-eyed, for the sentence to be carried out on her. And by his side, there would be his daughter, blond and frail and calculating, lately returned from the dead, and twice as vindictive. There would be no mercy, the Lady Julian knew that, no mercy, not even in times to come. Her memory would forever be tainted, her story always told by the child, the victorious child. There would be no telling of

33

how she'd tried to win Blanche's love; no recounting of her doomed attempts at understanding. Instead, there would always be her, the wicked stepmother, whose one wild attack would be made into many, as if by evil magic: and the child, innocent, suffering, frail, always lovely. An old story: that of the dragon, and the dragon-slayer. And everyone knew how such stories ended.

FRIENDSHIP

3

THE GIRL WHO LIVES AT NUMBER 54

BY BELINDA DORIO

The rain was relentless that night as it pelted onto my head and shoulders, the water beating hard enough to feel as if it was touching my bones. I gripped the window sill tighter as warm light flooded onto my dreary face. My nose resting on the sill as I pulled myself up to watch the family inside. Dinner was being put on the table and my stomach gave a painful lurch at the memory of steaming hot home-cooked food.

I'd been coming here for weeks now. My eyes were as hungry as my stomach when I watched them laughing happily together and every time I saw them. I wished I could go home. But I couldn't go back there and I knew it. The humiliation would drown me just as

36

surely as this rain would if I let it. That's all the world wants, is to drown you. The evening news, parents, and school – all they do is drown you in sorrows and misery, washing away your happiness.

The little girl named Lucy was already sat at the table. She must have been about ten years old but looked more like eight. She was a tiny little thing that looked like she could be blown over by the wind, but in her eyes was wisdom far beyond her years. I called her Mouse, just as I had called my little sister before I left home. Whenever I saw this little girl who lived at number fifty-four I felt the familiar pang of loss, because I missed my little sister more than I missed a warm bed and hot food in my stomach, and this girl reminded me so much of her. They had the same brightness in their eyes, the same intelligence that burned beneath the surface. But my sister was back in sunny Queensland while I rotted in the rain of Melbourne, and I suppose that's the way it should be. A grim smile tugged at my lips as I watched Mouse grab a few dinner rolls and wrap them in a napkin under the table. That would be my dinner tonight, and I thanked God again that I had found her for it wasn't just the food I craved, but ther company.

My hands began to cramp and my toes ached in

their wet socks, protesting being on tippy-toe for too long. I dropped from the window sill and crept around to the backyard in a way which I'm sure could be described as skulking and probably looked awfully suspicious. But I had to avoid the larger windows, so as not to alert Mouse's parents. I sat on the back steps of the house that belonged to this platonic family, and wondered what I was doing here. I didn't want to cause trouble and I certainly didn't want poor little Mouse to get too attached to me. She was such a sweet little kid, but what good would it do her to befriend a thieving bum? I pushed the thought from my head as I wrapped my arms around my chest, telling myself to stay until she brought dinner and willing the rain to stop. I didn't want Mouse to get caught up with me, but my grumbling stomach refused the thought of leaving without a meal. The little girl would bring me down food after her unsuspecting parents had gone upstairs to bed. She had been doing this for me since she caught me rifling through their garbage bin one night.

I had been starving and could barely think through the cramping in my stomach which was quickly turning to nausea. The world span as I tried to stand upright and I had fallen into something that went down with a loud crash. Spoiled food tumbled out of the bin and onto the side of the road and before I could really form the idea

38

in my mind, I was on my knees searching through the stinking remains for something remotely edible. She must have been drawn outside by the terrible ruckus I had made by tipping over their bin, but I would never forget the way she looked at me as she stood at the front of her house gripping the railing of the front patio. Her face hadn't shown fear or disgust - just great sympathy, and I watched it fill her eyes with a sadness I would have thought was beyond her years. When her parents informed her about homeless people, painting them as lazy and dangerous, I bet she pictured an overweight man with no teeth who smelt like the tip he was searching through. I'm sure she wasn't expecting a blonde haired teenage girl who wasn't even a decade older than herself.

The backdoor screeched open and jolted me from my thoughts as I jumped in surprise.

"Lou, it's only me." Mouse had to yell over the pounding rain as it bounced off the tin roof. I signalled for her to keep her voice down but she ignored me as she pushed her glasses back up her nose. She stood with the backdoor open, warm light shining around her. I marvelled at how mere light could seem so comforting and safe, but after spending over a year on the dark streets light seemed like a beautiful thing.

39

"Mum and Dad had to go visit my Grandad in hospital after dinner, why don't you come in for a bit? I convinced them it was ok to leave me home alone" She flashed me a mischievous smile that told me she thought she was quite clever to think of this. My heart gave a painful squeeze.

"I'm not sure kiddo, I'm ok out here" I gestured to the backyard but couldn't see more than a metre in front of me, as the rain continued to crash down in heavy grey waves.

Mouse pushed the door open wider and folded her arms stubbornly over her chest.

"Just come in, Lou. Nothing is going to happen" she said. My eyes kept darting to the door which promised safety and warmth. But I shouldn't. I should just stay out here.

"Really Lou! Come and get out of that rain, there is some meat from the roast left over that I can even heat up for you."

My tongue darted out to lick my lips before I could stop it. Maybe just for five minutes. Couldn't hurt – could it? With the thought of warm meat on my mind I followed Mouse into her home, water dripping off me

40

in rivulets.

I winced at the loud squelching noise my boots made on the polished floor boards as warm air from the ducted heating enveloped me like a blanket. Mouse instructed me to sit at the table in her authoritarian way and informed me she was going to fetch some towels and be right back, I nodded lamely and sat. She darted off, leaving me at the table with the leftover food and I faced the window that I'd been peeking through moments before. It felt strange to be on the other side of the picture and I fidgeted in my seat, thinking that this must be how caged animals felt. My stomach rumbled again and I quickly grabbed for the small dinner rolls sitting on the table and started shoving them in my pockets as another one found its way into my mouth, my eyes darting nervously around the house. I shouldn't be here, I shouldn't have come in.

I tried to still my hands, but after they were finished with the rolls I automatically started looking for something else to pick up.

What was taking Mouse so long?

I jumped up, hoping movement would take my mind off all the things I could steal from this house, all

41

the money I could get and how I could keep travelling, go anywhere, be anyone. That was how I had ended up in Melbourne; I had stolen and pawned enough items to get me a plane ticket. And here I was. My fingers drummed restlessly on my legs as sweat beaded on my forehead.

From peeking in the windows for a few weeks I had learnt that there was a large decorative bowl near the front door, which Mouse's family frequently dumped spare change into. I seemed to be on auto-pilot as my feet rushed me over to the bowl, no one would miss a bit of spare change. My boots squelched with me as my heart beat faster and faster and I felt clumsy in my cumbersome boots. The bowl of glittery change came into view. But when I reached the bowl I felt my heart still. Next to the bowl of change was a very fancy looking watch. My hands shook as I picked it up, inspecting the glittering stones in the face.

Diamonds, I was sure.

A rattle at the door and my heart leaped into my throat, squeezing my terrified yelp into more of a squawk.

"Luce, it's just us" a woman called "We forgot –"

A horrified scream as Mouse's mother saw me holding the watch in one hand, bread roll in the other. Pounding footsteps as her husband ran to the door.

"I- I'm sorry, I wasn't going to take it!" I stammered, slamming back into the bowl of change and spilling coins all over the floor. The gold watch clattered to the ground with them as I turned and ran for the backdoor, Mouse's Dad calling for his wife to phone the police. Mouse rounded the corner, towels forgotten. Her eyes behind her big glasses bright with panic as she reached out to me, but when I ran past her fingers only brushed my sleeve, and I sprinted away blindly until I finally pushed open the backdoor. My feet took me too fast and I nearly tripped down the back steps. I could hear Mouse desperately yelling at her father to stop as he chased after me.

The cold night air hit me in the face like a physical force and my lungs protested gulping the icy air after the warmth of indoors. I was running for my life one moment with eyes intent on the back fence, and the next I couldn't breathe, my face smashed into the mud on the ground and the breath knocked from me, a heavy weight crushing my chest as someone pinned me to the ground. I turned my head; Mouse's Dad's face was red with rage and exertion as he looked down on me, the

43

horrible grey rain a gruesome backdrop to his anger.

"How dare you break into our home!" he hissed.

I kicked and flailed but to no use, his hands clasped my arms like a vice and his knee jabbed painfully in between my shoulders.

"Dad!" screamed Mouse over the pelting rain.

"Dad, don't hurt her!" But the heavy man didn't listen, and tightened his grip as I screamed like a wounded animal.

"Dad, please! She's my friend!" At these words, the man's grip loosened for a moment in confusion and I used the opportunity to throw myself back as hard as I could. Miraculously he lost his hold for a moment and I scrambled frantically in the mud to get out from under him. More screaming and then finally I was running, I couldn't hear him chasing me but I didn't look back to check as my feet took me as fast as they could go, I grabbed the top of the fence and vaulted over, my feet slamming on the ground and I continued to run, the rain hitting my face like sharp needles as I escaped into the night.

Friend, she had said she was my friend.

44

Blue and red lights flashed as cops patrolled the streets, looking for me. A few were on foot and searching the park behind Mouse's house, correctly assuming that's where I lived. Though, my childhood adventures of climbing trees proved useful and the police searched half-heartedly as I watched from high above, nestled amongst the leaves of a gum tree. I dozed on and off whilst clutching the tree, one part of me worried I'd fall from the slippery branches as I slept, as another part of me hoped the fall would kill me. I wondered if little Mouse would care if I died and felt guilty when I hoped that she would. Memories of home flooded my mind as I huddled against the tree and I remembered why I had left in the first place:

The air had been warm, as it always was in North Queensland when I came home from school that day. I opened the front door and called out to my family but no one answered, they were always busy, always out somewhere. I tried to control my heart as its beat picked up in excitement. It was always now that I could snoop around the house without fear of exposure. I tried to resist the urge but always felt as if I would claw my own skin off if I didn't give in. I had started by looking in the usual places- Dads bedside table, Mums jar on top of the fridge, but there was little cash in the house that day. And it wasn't until months after that I would

45

realise my parents knew what I was doing, and now kept their savings on them or in the bank. I had gone down the hall and back into Mum and Dad's room when my eyes caught on Mums jewellery box, sitting innocently on her vanity table. Voices had urged me to just take a peek- 'what harm could it do?' they said. My hands felt clammy as I opened the lid, my fingers trailing over the gold and picking up a ring that Grandma had given her, as the diamonds glittered promisingly at me.

I denied taking it of course, even as my pocket had bulged with the money the pawn shop had given me, but my family knew of my sticky fingers and had correctly assumed I'd progressed from stealing cash to sentimental items, such as jewellery.

I couldn't deny the urge, sometimes I wouldn't even need the money, at seventeen I hadn't done drugs and I wasn't an alcoholic. It was just that I could take something that made me want to, and sometimes I didn't even remember doing it until I went to grab my wallet out of my pocket and found something else there. Stealing the ring signalled the end of my happy family life, and now when I reflect on my urge to steal I see it as a cry for attention- and attention it gave me, just not the right kind. I had been kicked out of home, my crime

46

too much for my parents to bear and they didn't want me having a bad influence on my little sister. I had been out of home for well over a year now, even though I knew all I needed to do was admit to what I had done, apologize and seek help. But I couldn't, the shame of my problem made me too embarrassed to return home. The voices weren't as bad as they had been before but sometimes they still came back, urging me to take something. But to return home and tell my family it wasn't my fault? That I had a problem? I worried that my parents had gone beyond caring for their thief of a daughter. They were probably glad I was out of their lives, not having a bad influence on their little girl – still holding out hope that one of their daughters would have a successful life. I remembered Mouse's Dad's face, contorted with rage. Why would my parents want me back?

The world plunged into and endless cycle of bleary lights, heavy rain and the ever-present darkness as the night tried to smother me. But soon the lights stopped flashing and I clambered down, too exhausted to move as I curled up beneath the tree to sleep, nestling in the mud like the pig I was. The rain refused to give me a break as it drizzled on and off on me throughout the morning. I rubbed at my bleary eyes and groaned as I rolled over and felt the beginnings of the bruises

47

developing along my torso. Children giggled and played in their wet weather gear at the park, their gleeful screams as they jumped in puddles pulling a smile from a part of me I thought was buried. Mud was caked all over my body and my jeans were stiff where it had dried. I tentatively touched my hair, once my pride and glory now matted and caked with mud also. I sighed sadly at the memory of my beautiful blonde hair, but my spirits soared when I patted down my jeans and found the remnants of a roll squashed inside one of the pockets. As I was scrapping the crumbs from my pocket, I tried not to let the mothers hurrying their children past with adverted gazes hurt my feelings. I wondered about little Mouse and hoped she didn't get into too much trouble for befriending a homeless kid who almost robbed her parents. I almost got up to go see her - to apologise, but the shame of being caught holding that sparkly watch kept me tethered to the tree. I was cold and shivering and I idly wondered whether I had hypothermia, then I remembered I didn't care.

When it was dark I ventured down to the lake at the back of the park to wash my clothes, well really it was more like a large dam. My jumper was scratchy as I peeled it off and the dry mud crackled and fell to the ground. It was then that I noticed the dim light across the lake, so faint through the soft rain that I almost didn't notice it. I quickly went back to the trees and moved cautiously closer to investigate, but all I could make out in the dark was a flash light on its side by the water. The light illuminated a patch of ominous looking reeds that loomed out of the murky depths. I moved a little closer and noticed a knapsack of bread and cheese near the flashlight that seemed as if it had been hastily left there. I moved closer again and noticed a disturbance in the water. What was it? Bubbles?

I ran to the water's edge, kicked of my boots and peeled off my still soaking socks before wading in up to my waist. I ignored the way the reeds stabbed at my bare feet and tried to ensnarl my legs as I searched in the darkness, the cold seeping back into my bones as if it was greeting an old friend. I stopped and held my breath in silence, my eyes scanning the surface of the water for movement when a splashing sound came just to my right, coming from thicker into the tall reeds. Without thinking I lunged towards the sound, not knowing whether I was about to give an eel a big fright and I thought about how stupid I must look as I jumped around in the water. But something hit my legs and my heart beat frantically as I dove my hands down into the inky darkness, and felt hair. I let out a small yelp in surprise and I felt around for the person's shoulders. When I had a good hold I began to yank them up, but

49

they seemed to be stuck on something. I managed to prop the persons head up out of the water and I went cold with shock when I saw the face. Mouse! Her glasses had fallen off and her lips were blue, hot panic chased away the shock and I dove down to free her legs. I couldn't see anything – it was too dark and the muddy water was thick and unforgiving as I tried to loosen the reeds around her foot, their sharp edges slicing my hands as I wrestled with them. I swam back up for a breath and cursed myself when I realised I had let Mouse drop under water again, so stupid! I held her small body up and supported her head again, realizing now that if I let her fall she would surely drown.

"Mouse!? It's Lou, can you hear me?" I asked desperately but her eyelids only fluttered a little. I wanted so much for her to open her eyes, to see the brightness in them shining back at me.

"Help! I screamed, help!" I held this poor little girl who had foolishly become my friend in my arms, too scared to let her go under the water again. Lack of food and sleep had my wiry body trembling to hold her up in the water and I heard shouts but the familiar feeling of failure loomed upon me as the world went as black as the water I struggled in.

50

The constant beeping noise in my ears was really getting on my nerves and my throat felt as if I had been eating sand for breakfast. I cracked an eye open to see a cup of water by the bed, and I reached for it eagerly but sharp pain stung my hands as they clutched the cup. I saw that thick scratches ran along my palms and blood blisters were popping up along my fingers. I looked around, startled. Last night's events were coming back to me in snippets - the torch light by the lake, the inky black water and Mouse's small frame in my arms, her lips turning blue. So small, so much like my little sister. And the failure, that feeling of failure that felt like it had knocked the wind from me. I looked around the room again with my head spinning, and I noticed there were a lot of bright colours floating around my bed. How odd. I blinked, confused as the colours merged with the images of the lake. When my vision cleared I saw that the colours were balloons, the type people give to their injured loved ones. I frowned as I looked at them and someone giggled.

Mouse stood by my bed in a hospital gown, and I realised where we were. My eyes scanned the child for damage but other than the dark smudges that underscored her big eyes, she looked ok, and I was happy to see that someone had found her glasses. She didn't quite look like my Mouse without them. Mouse's parents hovered like protective shadows over their daughter but I was glad to see that they didn't look like they wanted to kill me today, or was it tonight?

"Yes, they are for you" she said, echoing my doubts as I examined the bright balloons. I shook my head sharply to dislodge the strange fragmented thoughts still floating in my mind.

"Mouse? What happened? What on earth were you doing in the water?" I asked in a voice that sounded frantic, even too me. Mouse looked down, letting her hair hide her face and her fathers' brow puckered in a disapproving frown.

It was her mother who answered, in a sing-song voice that would seem more at home in a primary school class room than a hospital, her hands wringing themselves over and over.

"Lucy explained who you were after we found you in the house and, well we-"

"Banned Lucy from ever seeing you again" cut in the man in a matter-of-fact voice, his expression telling me he still wasn't impressed to have found me in his

52

home the way he did.

I nodded at this, ignoring the stab of hurt to my heart; I'd already presumed that would have happened. I was nothing but a mangy homeless girl with sticky fingers, but this still didn't explain why Mouse had almost drowned in the lake behind her house.

"We see now that this was not the best idea, but we didn't realise how strong Lucy's feelings were for you. She felt compelled to bring you food and seemed genuinely distressed when she couldn't" Mouse's Mum said. She sighed and patted Mouse on the head and little girl grinned at me.

"I waited for them to go to bed when I snuck out with some bread. I thought you had been sleeping in the park so I went down there. That's when I saw you by the lake" Mouse's cheeks flushed red before she continued. "I know it was silly but I wanted to surprise you. I was going to swim over and pop out of the water right in front of you!.."

"But you got stuck in the reeds?" I asked tentatively.

"Yeah" she said, her eyes darting down again.

"You silly thing Mouse, you didn't need to bring me anything! I don't want you feeling obliged to help me."

Mouse looked up sharply "But you are my friend! What am I suppose to do? Let you starve?" She looked so stern and serious that I let out a small chuckle. I patted her on the head as her mother had done, her concern warming my heart.

"I know, thank you Mouse. You have been a true friend to me" I smiled at her and thought how glad I was that I had been able to save her. For the first time in a long time, I felt proud.

Mouse's Dad cleared his throat "Ok, Luce, better let Louise get some rest now. You can catch up with her later." Mouse didn't seem impressed but gave my hand a squeeze and walked out of the room, I knew she must have been more exhausted than I was. I learnt that Mouse's parents had alerted the neighbours of her disappearance when they heard my shouts. We had both been dragged from the water and luckily Mouse hadn't needed CPR, as she coughed up the water she had swallowed and began to breathe on her own, and I had only blacked out for a moment from over-exertion before I was pulled from the lake.

"Seems us adults have a lot to learn about compassion" Mouses father mumbled as his wife nodded, eyes wide. "Louise, we cannot thankyou enough for saving our daughter and we know you put yourself at great risk to save her"

"It was my fault she was even going down there. I should never have let her care for me. It was wrong" I said quietly, my guilt pounding on my heart like a sledgehammer.

Mouse's father seemed to consider this, "No, I don't agree. It was Lucy that seems to have been drawn to you- for whatever reason, and from what she has told me you didn't take advantage of her in any way."

Her Mum cut in, "and we feel terrible about chasing you out of the house" she bit down on her lip as her hands continued to wring themselves.

"Is there something we could help you with? Like getting some new clothes, or maybe help you get a job? We know a lot of people in town."

I looked at these nice people, who just a day ago were chasing me around their house wanting to kill me. I sighed and my eyes seemed to drift shut on their own accord.

"Help me get home please. Just help me get home" I whispered.

Mouse and her parents had waved me off at the Melbourne airport domestic terminal and I had stepped out of the Cairns airport, the heat hitting me like a slap in the face - but I smiled, happy to be rid of Melbourne's often cold and dreary climate. I had one small bag of clothes that Mouse's parents had insisted on buying for me, along with the plane ticket. I touched my hair and inhaled the smell of strawberry shampoo with a smile as I sat in the back of a cab. I didn't know what I was going to say to my family, or whether they would listen, all I knew was that I was ready to change.

"Where to?" The cab driver asked as I smiled down at the photo of me and Mouse that I kept in my wallet. I may have saved her from drowning in that lake, but the girl who lived at number fifty-four had saved me with her kindness.

"Home" I said with a sigh of relief.

4

VISITING RIGHTS

BY GEORGE IVANOFF

"You're my knight in shining armour," smiled Virginia. "My protector. My champion. That's the way I think of you sometimes. My knight — saving me from loneliness, boredom and all the scary stuff that life is made of. I hope you don't mind."

The boy did not respond.

"I imagine you riding into my life on your snow-white charger, its breath steaming in the morning sunlight. Your amour is dazzlingly bright and difficult to look upon. You dismount with fairytale elegance and drop to one knee as you take my hand. Lifting your visor, you gaze meaningfully into my eyes, smile disarmingly and gently kiss my hand. And from that moment on, I am no one's but yours."

57

Virginia sat back in the armchair and gently shook her head.

"Silly isn't it?"

The boy did not answer.

"Oh well… strange things sometimes come into my mind."

Virginia yawned and stretched, then looked up at the clock.

"Oh shit," she exclaimed, jumping to her feet. "I'm late!"

She grabbed her schoolbag and dashed for the door.

***

The door creaked, ruining any hope Virginia had of sneaking unnoticed into the classroom. Heads looked up from textbooks.

The teacher sighed resignedly as he looked at Virginia and raised an eyebrow. She mouthed the word "sorry" and closed the door. He shook his head and indicated that she should sit down. Virginia looked at the floor and quickly weaved her way through the desks to the empty one beside Helen.

"Saved you a seat," said Helen.

"Thanks," Virginia answered as she sat down and

rummaged through her bag. She pulled out the textbook, laid it on the desk and began flipping through the pages.

"What page are we on?" she whispered.

"Ninety-five," answered Helen.

Virginia turned to the page and began reading. By the time she reached the bottom of the page, she still had no idea what she had been reading about. She wasn't even sure of the subject. She closed her eyes and took a deep breath.

"You've gotta stop seeing him," whispered Helen.

"I can't," answered Virginia.

"Keep missing classes and it's only a matter of time before you're in for a parent/teacher conference, you know," said Helen.

"Yeah," nodded Virginia, eyes still closed. "I know."

***

"Ya know, it is a bit weird," said Helen, sitting down on the bench next to Virginia.

"Yeah," conceded Virginia. "I know."

The two girls sat in silence for a few minutes, watching the bustle of recess take place around them. Virginia finally looked up at her best friend.

"I'm a bit weird," she said. "That's what most people think. So what's one more weird thing?"

"Suppose," answered Helen.

The silence dragged out between them, punctuated by the noise of the schoolyard.

"Oh come on, Hel," Virginia finally said. "Spit it out. You know you want to."

Helen looked up at her friend. There were dark circles under Virginia's hazel eyes. Her normally pretty face, framed by chestnut curls, looked in desperate need of a good night's sleep.

"Go on," said Virginia. "This silence is worse than anything you could say."

"Oh, Virg!" Helen looked into her best friend's eyes, concern etched over every feature. "I'm just worried about you, that's all. You spend all your spare time with him. And… and… well, you seem to be spending more and more time with him. You go there before school. You go there after school. You've been late every day this week."

"He's my friend," said Virginia.

"I know that. But… well… there's a line between friendship and… and obsession, I suppose. And… well… I hate to say it… but… I think you've crossed it."

Virginia shrugged.

"It's not just what I think. I'm your friend. I understand." Helen paused for a moment, looked down at her feet as she dug a heel into the grass, and then continued. "Well… actually, I don't really understand… but I'm trying to. Honestly! You know… I really am. But…"

"I know," said Virginia. "It's weird."

Helen continued to stare at the grass. She had dug a sizable hole with the heel of her shoe. She now played around the edges with the toe of her shoe as she tried to choose her next words.

"People are talking," she finally said, deciding there was no delicate way of putting it. "You're the hottest topic of gossip around the school."

Virginia nodded as she looked out across the school grounds. Helen was right. She knew it. She knew it from the way the other kids looked at her. She knew it from the way the teachers treated her. She knew it from the things people didn't say.

"I don't care about gossip," said Virginia defiantly. "I don't care what people think!"

Helen looked up at her friend. They stared at each other for a few minutes.

"Oh, okay," Virginia said, looking away. "I do care."

She looked around at the other kids. Kids playing.

Kids talking. Kids mucking about. Kids interacting with each other. Then she looked back at Helen.

"But I care more about Ewan than I do about what they all think… or say."

Helen nodded.

"I feel content when I'm around him," Virginia continued. "Peaceful… and… happy. He makes me happy."

The silence descended again. Virginia turned her attention back to the other kids in the school grounds, and Helen returned to her hole, kicking at it a little more.

A few minutes later Helen muttered:

"Um… can I ask you a stupid question?"

"Sure."

"What do you do?"

"Huh?"

"What do you do while… you know… while you're there with him?"

Virginia laughed. "Well, I talk to him, of course. What do you think I do?"

"I dunno," Helen shrugged. "Knit… or something."

"Knit?" Virginia burst out laughing.

Helen looked up at her friend, watched her laughing, and then started laughing herself.

"Yeah, well," said Helen, between giggles. "Maybe

you're like… like this closet knitter." She almost fell over with laugher, clutching at her sides. Other kids stared at them as they passed. "Maybe it's like… something you keep hidden from the world… and only do when you're alone… or like… when…"

The girls' laughter trailed off.

"Or when…" said Virginia sombrely, "or when I'm with him."

Helen looked back down at the hole.

***

Virginia walked silently to her next class with Helen. As they passed a group of boys in the corridor, one of them called out.

"Hey Virgin-ia!" They all burst into childish giggles.

"Just ignore them," said Helen resolutely, not even looking in their direction.

The girls walked on.

One of the boys broke from the group and chased after them.

"Come on, Virgy," he said. "We were only kiddin'."

He skipped ahead of them and started to walk backwards, a few steps in front.

63

"Hey, I was wondering if you're busy today, after school?" he persisted. "Maybe you could go out with me?"

"Sorry," said Virginia, quickening her pace. "I've got plans."

"Oh, come on," he quavered in a mock-pleading voice, holding both hands on his chest, over his heart. "I've gotta be more fun than your boyfriend." His face broke into a grin.

"Push off!" declared Helen, shoving past him.

"Hey," the boy shouted after them as he stopped in the corridor. "I can just lie there and not say anything if you like."

The other boys caught up to him, and they all started laughing again, one of the boys giving him a high five.

Virginia quickened her pace even more, looking steadfastly down at the floor, trying hard to hold back tears. I will not cry in front of those pigs, she thought to herself.

Helen flipped them the finger over her shoulder and she hurried to catch up with her friend.

"Oooooo!" The boys chorused amidst more laughter.

"You okay?" Helen asked quietly.

Virginia nodded hurriedly. "Let's just get to class."

***

When the lunch bell sounded, Virginia shoved her books into her bag and dashed out of the class without waiting for Helen. She went straight to the back end of the school and sat down in the secluded corner. There she ate her lunch in silence.

She was half way through lunch before Helen found her.

"Why'd you ditch me?" she asked, sitting down next to her.

Virginia shrugged.

"Worried about what I might say?"

Virginia shrugged again.

"Well, you're probably right to be worried… 'cause I am here to talk to you. And I'm worried. I'm worried about you." Helen paused, waiting for a response. When none came, she continued. "It's not healthy. You're becoming obsessed. It's affecting the rest of your life… and that's not good. It's taking over your life. And it's giving ammunition to the school idiots."

"He's my friend," said Virginia. "I like him. I like talking with him."

"Oh, honey," said Helen. "How could you possibly

talk with him? At best, you're talking at him. At worst… you're just talking to yourself."

"It's not like that," protested Virginia.

"This isn't a fairytale," pleaded Helen. "You can't wake him with a kiss. And you're not going to ride off into the sunset to live happy ever after."

Virginia looked away.

"You can't go on like this forever. It's got to stop sooner or later. And the sooner it is, the better it'll be for you."

"It is going to stop," said Virginia, looking up to meet her friend's eyes. Her own eyes slowly filled with tears. "It's going to stop today."

"Oh shit," said Helen, suddenly realising what she meant. "I'm sorry Virg… I didn't realise."

"It's okay Hel. I'm ready… I think."

"Come here," said Helen, opening her arms and wrapping them around her friend. "I am sorry. I really am."

***

Virginia struggled through the rest of the school day. She was out the front gates and down the road within minutes of the end-of-school bell. As she sprinted for the tram stop, a familiar green BMW pulled up in front of her, horn blaring.

"Here we go again," sighed Virginia as she opened the front passenger door, threw her bag in and followed it.

"Where do you think you're going?" asked a severe looking woman, the layers of make-up doing little to disguise the fact that she was on the wrong side of fifty.

"You know where I'm going, Mum."

"Yes I do," answered the woman sternly. "You're coming home."

"Mum, we've been through this before," sighed Virginia.

"Yes we have. And you're coming home right now. You are going to do your homework. You are going to help me with dinner. And you are going to sit in the lounge room and watch some mindless television. We are going to be a normal family tonight."

"We can play Happy Families tomorrow, Mum," said Virginia, fiddling with her bag's shoulder strap. "Today, I've got to go and visit Ewan."

"Oh for goodness sake, Virginia," the woman burst out. "You have gone to visit him every day for the past three weeks."

She grabbed a packet of cigarettes from the dashboard and fumbled with them until she had one in her trembling hand. She stuck it in her mouth and began looking for the lighter.

"I wish you wouldn't smoke, Mum," said Virginia. "It's not good for you."

"Well, I wish you'd stop visiting that boy," said the woman still searching for the lighter, a little more frantically now. "But you still do."

She finally gave up on the lighter, snatched the cigarette from her mouth and threw it at the windscreen. It bounced off the glass and landed on the dashboard next to the packet.

"Why?" she demanded. "Why do you keep visiting him? You barely knew him. Is it guilt?"

"No!" protested Virginia.

"Because it's not your fault," insisted her mother, "just because he was coming to see you when it happened."

"I know that!" Virginia's voice rose.

"So why then?" Her mother's voice rose to match hers. "It's not as if you can have any sort of relationship with someone who can't even…"

Her voice trailed away. Anger and frustration were replaced with a dawning realisation.

"Is that it?" she asked in a whisper. "Is this your way of playing safe? After all, he can't do anything, so he sure as hell can't hurt you. For goodness sake, Virginia, you're hiding. And you can't hide forever."

"You just don't understand, do you?" Virginia shook her head. "You never even try."

Virginia turned and reached for the door handle.

"Don't you get out of this car," her mother demanded, her fingers fumbling for the auto-lock control. "Don't you dare!"

Virginia opened the door seconds before her mother's fingers found the control. She jumped out of the car and slammed the door as hard as she could. There was a tram at the stop, just about to leave. Virginia ran for it, hopping on board as the doors closed. She could still hear the car horn blaring impotently as the tram pulled away.

***

Virginia tossed her school bag to the floor and slumped into the chair beside the bed. She was still fuming over the confrontation with her mother. Closing her eyes, she took a long, deep breath, held it, and then slowly exhaled. As she felt herself calming down, she opened her eyes and looked at Ewan.

"Hi," she smiled, her face lighting up. "Good to see you."

She reached forward and grabbed her bag. After rummaging around inside, she pulled out a magazine and held it up. A red and yellow sports car zoomed across a racetrack at high speed.

"I found this on the tram seat after school," she shrugged. "I know you're into that sort of thing, so I saved it for you."

She carefully placed it onto the bedside table, nudging a vase of flowers to one side.

"Hope you weren't too bored today." She got to her feet and approached the bed. "I certainly wasn't." She gently smoothed down the sheets at the end of the bed. "School just keeps rolling right along." She casually strolled to the foot of the bed, picked up the chart and examined it as if she actually knew what all the notes meant. "I'd rather be here, of course. With you." She replaced the chart and glanced over at the monitor. The only thing she understood was the heart rate, steadily beeping away. "But people seem to be freaked out enough as it is, with me coming here before and after school." She walked back around the bed and sat on the edge, inches from Ewan's hand. "Even Helen. She's trying to understand, but even she's freaked out." Virginia looked at Ewan. "Am I weird for coming here?" She looked at him, lying helplessly in the bed, connected to monitors and drips and machines that breathed for him. "Is there something wrong with me for wanting to spend time with you?"

Ewan didn't respond.

"Helen thinks I'm obsessed. Mum thinks I'm either feeling guilty or hiding from life. Everybody's talking about us. The new boy and the school weirdo. Everybody's got a theory. There's even a bit of graffiti in the girl's loo suggesting that the accident was a way for you to avoid going out with me. Stupid people!"

She shook her head slowly.

"No one seems to think it may simply be because I like you."

Virginia smiled.

"And I do like you."

She ran a hand over the sheets again, smoothing them down even though there were no creases.

"When I was younger I used to have an imaginary friend. I used to talk to him all the time… about all sorts of stuff. And sometimes he'd talk back. Tell me things I needed to hear." Virginia sighed. "But he wasn't real."

She continued to smooth her hand over the sheets.

"You know, sometimes I imagine that you're talking back to me… with me. I know you're not… but I like to pretend… sometimes. Pretend that you're going to be okay. That your eyes will snap open. That you'll sit up, take my hand and…"

"Excuse me," said the nurse, poking her head

round the door. "Mrs Long is waiting for you in the foyer."

"Thanks," said Virginia, and the nurse disappeared. "Almost time." She patted Ewan's hand. "I'll be back soon."

She got to her feet and walked to the door. She stopped momentarily and turned back.

"Every day I hope. Every day… I hope for a miracle… for a fairytale ending. Could I wake you from your slumber with true love's kiss?"

Calmly she left the room, walked over to the foyer and sat down on the hard plastic chair next to Ewan's mother. The woman looked up with sad, empty eyes.

Dead, thought Virginia, dead eyes.

Suddenly the woman grabbed at Virginia's hand with a fevered desperation. She clutched it as if her life, her very existence, depended on it.

"I can't," she sobbed. "I just can't be there." She held on to Virginia's hand. "I'm sorry." Her voice was pleading, begging, threatening to break. "You understand, don't you?"

Virginia nodded.

"Thank you," whispered Mrs Long as she began to rock back and forth in her seat. "Thank you. Thank you. Thank you."

Absolution, thought Virginia, that's all it takes for

72

some.

***

"I think I'm ready to let go," said Virginia, as the doctors and nurses bustled around Ewan. "To go on with life… without you."

Virginia was surprised at how quickly it all happened. Machines were disconnected and wheeled away. Tubes and drips removed.

"I'll leave you alone with him," said the last of the nurses as she closed the door behind her.

"I'll miss you," said Virginia. "I really will. Who will I talk to now?"

Virginia sighed — a long, resigned, accepting sigh.

"I wish I could have known you longer. You were kind to me when few others were. You didn't hit on me when I was fragile. And you asked me out at the very moment I decided I was ready. It's like you know me. Not just the things I like and the music I listen to and stuff like that. It's like you really know me. Understand me. Me. The deep, hidden me that no one else sees. The me who's sometimes scared of the world. The me who's yearning to burst free, to dance in the rain and run barefoot through the grass, to bask in the moonlight and name the stars, to look into the eyes of my soul

73

mate and understand, really, truly, understand love. That's who you are to me. My knight. My day. My… everything."

"But now they tell me it's time to let you go. Go where, I wonder? Ride off into the sunset on a white horse, your armour shining so brightly I can barely see. They tell me I should say goodbye…" Virginia choked back tears. "Well… I won't. I refuse! Instead…"

Virginia leant over and brushed her lips against his cheek.

"Till we meet again," she whispered.

As the tears welled in her eyes and her vision blurred, Virginia saw Ewan's eyelids flutter.

She pulled back and gasped.

Had she seen his eyelids flutter?

She wanted to see his eyelids flutter.

But she knew that was impossible — no matter how much she wanted it. Fairytale endings did not happen in real life.

Virginia picked up her schoolbag and slung it over one shoulder. For a moment she contemplated the flowers on the bedside table — should she take them home with her? She could put them in a vase in her bedroom and watch them slowly die over the course of a few days. She picked up the magazine instead.

"I hope you don't mind if I take this with me," she

said quietly, shoving it into her bag.

As she headed for the door, a melancholy smile gently tugged at the corners of her mouth.

"And I hope you don't mind if I still talk to you from time to time."

ROMANTIC LOVE

5

TO HAVE LOVED AND LOST

BY RACHEL PLUM

It's all well and good for Shakespeare to write it's better to have loved and lost than to have loved at all but, to my knowledge, Shakespeare was never a widow. I've loved and I've lost but I've also lost something else and I don't know how to get it back.

The knock at the door startles me, despite its mild volume. I know it's Vanessa before she speaks.

'Phil? Are you there?'

Good question. I open the door to Vanessa's warm smile. I'm amazed how she manages such a cheery disposition.

Realising my face probably looks like *I've* been

stood up, I make an effort at a smile but smiles shouldn't take effort. Vanessa's a good sport and doesn't wince at my strained expression. Further to that, there isn't even the slightest lowering of her eyebrows to betray pity.

'You were supposed to meet me at the Bean Scene half an hour ago. What happened?'

'I guess I lost track of time.' My eyes drop and examine the carpet.

I met Vanessa six weeks ago at the Bean Scene coffee shop, downstairs from my apartment, and we've met each other at the same time every week since.

'No problem,' she beams. 'Let's take it again from the beginning. I'll meet you at the Bean Scene in five minutes.' I smile effortlessly this time.

I walk into the Bean Scene and, as the smell of freshly ground arabica beans hits my nostrils, I locate Vanessa waving from a booth in the back. The familiarity brings comfort.

I raise a hand to acknowledge Vanessa and order our favourites from the counter; a hot chocolate for her and a vanilla cappucino for me.

As I hand Vanessa her coffee she grins from ear to ear. 'Mmm, my favourite.'

I'd like to feel the same enthusiasm but it's not

78

forthcoming.

'Mmm,' I mumble, rubbing my stomach unconvincingly.

Vanessa overlooks my flatness but I can't help feeling everything between her and me is slipping through my fingers.

'Guess wha-aat?' Vanessa lyricises.

'What?' I ask. I try to smile with my eyes but feel the tension in my face.

'You know how your birthday's coming up...?'

'It's hard to forget with you around,' I say dryly.

The topic of birthdays came up in discussion when we first met, and she's brought up mine for the last three weeks. Each time she has prompted me to do something special but each time I've said something non-committal and planned nothing.

'Well, hold onto your seat.'

I grip my seat, feigning concern I may be knocked off it by her news.

'We're going away for the weekend.'

I don't know what to say.

'Don't give me that look,' she coaxes.

I'm giving a look?

'I know you've got nothing planned,' she continues. 'Besides, you could use a weekend away.'

'What about Matilda?' I ask.

79

Oh yeah, I have a daughter named Matilda. She's 6. Her mother's name was Jessica and she has Jessica's looks. She's as smart as a whistle... or however the saying goes.

'She'll come too. We'll each have our own room, at- Hold onto your seat again.'

I hold my seat, with less theatrics this time.

'Beautiful Port Macquarie.' Vanessa accentuates her announcement with an elegant flurry of arms and hands, like a game show model highlighting the car.

My eyes drift to where Vanessa is gesturing as I take in the news, until my thoughts are interrupted by a lady sitting with friends at the next table.

I'm inadvertently staring at them.

'Sorry," she offers. "We're not Port Macquarie.'

The drive from Sydney to Port Macquarie is semi-relaxing. Sophie's intermittent bouts of the wheels on the car go round and round don't help. It's cute at first but the novelty wears off for me long before it does for Matilda. I spare her the rendition of Daddy's brain goes throb throb throb on loop in my head. Vanessa drives, which gives me a chance to sit back and enjoy the scenery. My thoughts wander as I look out the window. I think about my life with Sophie and how Vanessa fits into it. Then my mind turns to Laura and anything I think I've worked out about Vanessa fades away.

Our holiday apartment is a cheery blue and yellow beachy affair.

Matilda runs from room to room, deciding which bedroom to claim.

'So what do you think?' Vanessa asks.

'It's nice.'

'It's more than nice.' Vanessa squeezes my arm in excitement. 'It's great!'

'It *is* great. And this room is mine!' Matilda calls, standing atop the queen size bed in the master bedroom.

Vanessa pulls a brochure out of her hand bag. 'Guess what we're doing toda-aay.' There is that sing-song tone again. The sofa is too far away, so I take the news standing.

'We are going to- Drum roll!'

There is an awkward moment when I'm not sure if she is saying drum roll in place of performing one, announcing a drum roll to come, or-

She gestures for me to do a drum roll.

I putter one out on my thigh.

'A waterfall!'

I can tell Vanessa was expecting more excitement from me.

She looks like she's about to ask me what is wrong

when Matilda chirp's in. 'Mummy loved waterfalls. We used to go to them on the weekends sometimes. And mummy's very favourite was called Sampson Falls. What's this waterfall called?'

Vanessa looks at the name in the brochure: Sampson Falls, then up at me.

'Sampson Falls isn't the biggest waterfall we went to but mummy said it was her most specialest.'

'Really? Her most specialist?' Vanessa kneels down to Matilda's level. 'I have to talk to your daddy. So, do you want to watch cartoons?' She looks at the time on her phone. 'Dora the explorer is about to start.'

'How do you know?'

'I've got nieces.'

'Yay. Dora.' Matilda runs to the sofa.

With Matilda entertained, Vanessa meets me in the kitchen area.

'You didn't mention that you and Matilda's mum used to go to Sampson Falls.'

'I didn't think it would be relevant.'

'Well, it is. I brought you here to relax and get away from it all, so you could go back to Sydney mentally refreshed.' She frowns. 'Now I've probably just made it worse.'

I knew it. 'Made what worse.'

'Excuse me?'

'You said *made it worse*. That implies something is wrong.'

'I didn't mean that.'

'But you said it.'

'I didn't mean there is anything wrong with you. But don't you think you could feel *more right*?'

I don't answer.

'When was the last time you did something on par with a *most specialest* moment?'

'You're not Jessica.' Too harsh. But she's not.

'I-'

'Matilda. Let's go.'

'Are we going to the waterfall now daddy?'

'Yes.'

I stuff towels and swimmers into a backpack and usher Matilda to the door.

'Why are we going without Vanessa?'

Why *are* we going without Vanessa?

'We just are,' I say, closing the door.

At the falls, Matilda and I swim around.

She stands on a rock she used to jump off into the water. Last year, I would stand in the water a few metres from the rock so she could grab hold of me after she jumped but Matilda's a bit older now and I don't

83

have to be as close.

'Mummy- I mean daddy. Look.'

She used to call out to Jessica to watch her jump.

We swim and play some more, then Matilda asks me 'Is Vanessa going to be my second-mummy?'

'Do you want Vanessa to be your mummy?'

'Not my mummy,' she explains. 'My second-mummy. Mummy was my mummy and Vanessa can be my second-mummy. Little girls like to have mummies. And second-mummies.'

'Is that right?'

'Uh huh. But little girls don't like third-mummies,' she warns. 'Not while they still have a second-mummy. And Vanessa would be a nice second-mummy.'

'She would. Wouldn't she?'

When we get back to the holiday apartment, Vanessa has a home-cooked lasagne in the oven.

'Hi Vanessa,' Matilda calls from the door. 'What's that yummy smell?'

'Hi Matilda. It's lasagne and it will be ready soon. How was your day?'

'Good. I'm going to play in my room before yummy dinner!' She runs into the master bedroom and leaps onto the bed.'

'How was *your* day,' Vanessa asks.

84

'Well, it started out with some good scenery and some great singing…'

She smiles.

'Then I made a mistake, and I'm sorry.'

'That's okay. You don't need to-'

'Yes, I need to apologise. I made a big mistake. After that, I played and swam with my daughter. We talked. I think, now, everything is going to be more right. You are one of the two most specialest people in my life right now. I hope you will stay around to keep being part of it.'

I already lost mummy. I don't want to lose second-mummy.

6

HOLIDAYS AT THE LAKE

BY JAMES CROWN

Do you know what it's like to have that one girl who is the only one for you? It can't just be any girl. I'm talking about the one you are so besotted with it doesn't occur to you to think about any other girl. The girl you would give up everything for and happily live out the rest of your lives together in a little hut in the middle of nowhere. I did for eight years. Well, for eight Januaries. But life has a habit of getting in the way. *Why do we let that happen?* She is moving away to take up a prestigious scholarship. But I'm getting ahead of myself. I'll take you back to the beginning, where something beautiful started.

Every summer, the Walker family and the Stuart family would get away to Prescott Lake for the summer. I'm Brad Walker and these summer getaways started when I was 10. Her name: Karly Stuart. We were born two months apart. Karly's birthday was always in the week before we arrived at the lake. That first time, I hadn't wanted to go away because there was no TV and I was banned from taking my handheld computer games. This was back in the 1988 at a time when a game called Jump Man was the biggest craze among my school friends, occupying us until Sonic and Mario came along.

The one consolation for my lack of TV and computer games was that I convinced my parents to let me bring my best friend Jake Foster along. They had talked to his parents and they were more than happy for the break because Jake's family lived above the corner shop in my street and they saw each other all the time. The prospect of spending a month out at a lake was much more palatable with Jake there to pass the time with.

Arriving at the lake that first January, Jake and I spied some good climbing trees and vowed to make the best tree house we had ever seen while we were there. It seemed such a noble goal at the time. The best tree house we had ever seen! I had only seen two but that was beside the point. Once we had settled in and were allowed to play, Jake and I went straight to the trees we had seen as we arrived.

One tree was the perfect candidate for our grand tree house endeavour. We found Karly Stuart climbing in that tree. We soon made her a partner in the tree house. I would like to say it was love at first site, but to be honest we brought her in on the tree house because we didn't want her in the way of something so important to two ten year olds. Plan B was to throw pinecones at her. My life may have been very different if the pinecones had been plan A.

We made the tree house and it was good. It was stable enough but not all that pretty. It was hobbled together from snapped branches and sticks but, as we had intended, it was the best we had ever seen. At least, we thought so. Karly helped with the construction. Not as often as Jake and I did but when she helped she was industrious and understood the importance of making the construction stable.

We spent many hours in the tree that January. Swinging, climbing to the top, laying in the shade. To us it was perfection. Jake and I built several more tree houses throughout 1988 but none compared to that January tree house at the lake. Maybe it was because the first one still had novelty. Maybe our tastes in comfort had grown more sophisticated. Maybe it was a combination of things. But I think Karly's presence may have been part of it. Girls were not allowed in that year's later efforts because by ten and a half it was a widely held practice that boys in our grade had to maintain a pretence that girls had cooties and vice versa. I don't think any of us really believed in cooties but failing to put on a good show of aversion to catching cooties resulted in ridicule and being branded a cooties carrier for the day. No-one wanted to be a cooties carrier.

However, our innocence to the dangers of cooties had earned us a January acquaintance we regarded as a friend. But we would not have admitted it at school that year. This friendship paid unexpected dividends the following January at the lake.

The Walker family arrived before the Stuarts in the summer of 1989. Brad and I had convinced our parents to let Brad come with my family to the lake each year as a regular arrangement. Arriving this time, the tree house looked much more ramshackle and less impressive than we had thought. Some of it had degraded over the past year but it still held its shape. Nevertheless, we still had a fondness for it.

When the Stuarts four wheel drive pulled up, Karly called out to us through the window. We ran over. Karly had asked her parents for wood, nails, hammers and a saw for her birthday. This was a whole new January with a whole new tree house! This was also the beginning of a whole new appreciation for Karly. At just over 11, I still had another year of cooties pretence ahead but I didn't think of Karly as a girl. She wasn't like some girl at school. She was Karly.

We piled boards by the tree, unloading them ourselves as the adults unloaded everything else from the four wheel drive. It was at some point during the process of hauling the boards to the trees and tearing down the old tree house that I decided I would hold Karly's hand before January was done. It couldn't be a handshake but had to be a handholding of mutual consent, with both of us knowing that we were officially holding hands. This was not something that was entered into lightly. Such a bold move could make anyone subject to endlessly creative and evolving schoolyard rumours of what they got up to sitting in a tree. If it got out that I'd spent the summer with my fellow hand-holder I'd be toast. Further, if news of a handholding knock back got out I would be subject to the rumours without the benefit of any handholding. I was in dangerous territory. I had to get it right.

I kept my ambition to myself. It was too sensitive a topic to share even with Jake. No-one would have any idea of my intentions until the moment was right and that was the way I liked it. Meanwhile, we agreed that a design was in order before getting to work. We spent an afternoon drawing all manner of fanciful designs. Our early efforts were well beyond our skills and resources to build but a few more rounds of designs and some adult technical advice lead us to a floor and roof frame design to give us a safe, stable floor and a weather-resistant roof utilising a tarp.

More than once in the first few days I had found myself looking at Karly's hands as we sawed, passed boards up the tree and banged nails. When she got a splinter, I was more concerned than her because of the potential spanner it could throw into my plan. That tree house was our new standout best ever. The three of us had each other, our wooden floor and our tarp roof. We wanted for nothing that January.

The plan didn't play too much on my mind because I had settled on what I was going to do. I kept my personal belongings as packed up as possible so that on the last day when Jake spent an hour packing I could sneak away and get in some handholding. No-one from school would have to know. I reasoned we would leave before Jake could find out from Karly and she wouldn't bother to tell him after a year had passed. My plan was airtight.

When the last day came, my plan was in good shape. Jakes belongings looked like they had exploded into every corner of the room and mine were neatly packed. I casually strolled out of the room, not letting on my urgency, but as soon as I passed round the doorframe I rushed to find Karly. The Stuarts' four wheel drive was gone but my parents informed me Karly's father had just taken a trip down a local side road before they left, to see what was down there.

I found Karly swinging on the tree and knew the moment was upon me. It was then or never. Or at least then or the next year, which seemed like an eternity away. I invited her to sit in the tree house a last time before we left. Sitting on the boards under the tarp, I asked her, almost like I was proposing marriage, 'Will you hold hands with me?' She understood the gravity of my request. She was a little taken back but wearing the biggest smile I had ever seen. Karly and I held hands for what seemed like blissful hours, but must have been about 15 minutes, before her father returned in the four wheel drive and her mother called her.

Eight years on, with Karly heading overseas, we will probably only see each other once a year. It won't be for a month but probably from time to time when she returns to the country for summer holidays. We have been used to that and it has not gotten between us but it will be different from now on. Our love has only ever been Platonic but it has been love and I do not know what future that love has, as life intervenes. I do know that I will always remember our summers together and my first true love.

AMBITION

7

KIMBERLEY FORTUNE

BY REKHA AMBARDAR

Prancing flames from the old stone fireplace threw jagged, taunting lights like the aurora borealis across the cavernous interior of the drawing room of Thornton Croft, while outside a white moon etched shadows on the yew hedge skirting the grounds.

Gordon Dunlap patted the upturned faces of the great danes, Drago and Cinnabar, then faced his younger brother, Clive, recently returned from Kimberley, ostensibly a wealthy man from his diamond mining enterprises there.

"You had better accept it, Gordy" he said, affecting a grandiose pose by the fireplace, a gold watch and chain strung on the vest of his suit. Since his return he had adopted the attire of the landed gentry in Sussex, parts of which boasted of their ancestral property, with Thornton Croft, their country estate, resplendent as its

95

crowning glory. "Viola and I plan to marry and there's nothing you can do to stop us, as I am sure you understand, dear brother." The "dear" sounded like a veritable taunt for at no time had Clive understood another's pain.

Their mother, long deceased, had doted on her younger son; his golden curls and merry blue eyes could capture the susceptible heart of any female, old or young. Gordon was the serious responsible one, tending the sheep shearing business and overseeing the farmlands.

"I can hardly stop you," Gordon said, determined not to show that he was sick at heart, for he had met the lady first at the home of a count whose wife had introduced Gordon to her sister, Voila.

"You had your chance before I arrived, brother," Clive said languidly. "All's fair and all that sort of thing, and may the best man win."

"I am not your rival, Clive, merely your brother," Gordon said wearily, remembering the day, ten years ago when Clive set out to seek his fortune like some character from a Grimm brothers story. He went not into a forest or to seek the hand of a fair damsel, but to a far country, away from the placid greenery of the British Isles. His wanderlust led him straight to the Kimberlite dykes in the diamond-mining town that bore its name.

The diamond fervour had started in 1866, some seventy-five years ago, when a shepherd boy found a white pebble in the Orange River. The white pebble was none other than a twenty-five carat diamond awaiting discovery in its pristine condition.

When Clive left, he borrowed against his inheritance, their father still being alive. From that moment on, the younger son was never to be heard from again until he made his fortune, and returned to Sussex only to find that their father had passed on and Gordon was the owner of the enterprise.

In the meantime, Viola filled Gordon's dull working days with her feminine charm, calling at Thornton Croft, accompanied by her sister, Cassandra, on cold, rainy afternoons. He would trudge in from the farm, stamping his galoshes outside the servants' entrance and find Viola and Cassandra waiting in the drawing room.

So the days grew into meaningful ones for him, each day that Viola visited with her sister in attendance.

Then one day, Viola came alone.

"What, no Cassandra today?" Gordon said in jest, delighted that he could have Viola to himself for and hour, perhaps showing her the farm and the animals.

"No. Cassandra is indisposed with a bad cold,"

97

Viola said. "She asked our housekeeper, Mrs. Meeker, to accompany me. She will be back to fetch me in a cab."

They spent a glorious hour talking of the new inventions, the machines that one could look through to make things look larger, new ways of farming. Viola helped with her sister's young children, and was a doting aunt. Did she not want children of her own? he ventured to ask. Yes, she said, she would like children of her own very much someday when she met the right man.

That day Gordon vowed that he would be that man and he asked if he could call on her at her sister's home.

Seeing his brother standing in front of him now jolted his thoughts back to the present and it hit Gordon hard how drastically things had changed.

"I've strived many years to be where I am today." Clive said and moved toward the long door that opened out to the grounds. He stood staring out into the distance where tall elms dotted the end of the lawn as far as the eye could see. "The long hours in the searing heat with the other miners, never knowing if I would come out alive." His breath palpitated with the words as they came out, punctuating them with heavy emotion. "If you found a diamond pebble and the man next to you saw it, you could be killed the next minute."

"But you were not killed." Gordon admired his brother's staying power despite a vocation fraught with danger. Even though he had been the spoiled one in the family, Clive had persevered in his diamond mining mission. His brother exuded bravado as naturally as a mole dug holes in the ground and Gordon watched mesmerized.

"Do you know how hard life is in the craggy wilds of the kopjes and the barren mountains? Nothing but wide stretches of stone and gravel, hidden by thin vegetation. And the heat. The maddening heat." Clive let out a sigh and plunged his fingers through his hair in a frustrated movement, a gesture Gordon had witnessed many times before. He strode over to Gordon and stopped in front of him, a look of defiance in his eyes. "What do you know about hardship?"

"Spare me the dirge, brother." Now Gordon was the one with the sneer in his voice. "I have worked just as hard, tending to business, settling the debts that Father left, ministering to Mother's needs as she lay ill. Where were you then?"

Gordon got up and walked to the long door, turned and strode back to face his brother. "Now that you are back, you can help me with the business," Gordon said.

"What?' Clive snorted and then preened himself in front of the mirror that hung adjacent to the fireplace.

"Run the business? Are you mad?" he spat out. "I wouldn't last one day doing that after having lived in a tin hut or a kraal. After seeing sordid avarice and danger in the life lived there, I would die of boredom."

"Why did you return then?" A swell of irritation seeped into Gordon's tone and he was powerless to stop it. Clive's arrogance never ceased to annoy Gordon. Still Gordon had to remind himself that Clive was his kith and kin, and that an older brother must be patient with the younger.

"To claim what inheritance I might have."

"Are you not a wealthy man? What would you want with such a pittance as this?" Gordon asked, puzzled.

"It is the principle of the thing. As the younger son I have come to claim my inheritance." He flopped on the old leather armchair and thrust one long leg over the side.

"What will you do with the money from the diamond operations?" Gordon asked, piqued.

"Invest it in the new railway locomotive industry," Clive said sounding maddeningly complacent. "These are dynamic times, brother, with new inventions on the horizon each day. Any one of these could be a good investment for my money."

Obviously Clive had his future planned like a czar

while Gordon toiled in trying to keep the farmland replenished and the livestock fed.

Mrs. Kemper, their housekeeper from the days of their parents, brought in the tea, toast and butter on the well-worn wooden tray. No frills and fripperies ever decorated their routine – they had lived Spartan, frugal lives.

"Tea and toast," the good woman announced and placed the tray on the low oakwood table in front of the sofa upholstered in sturdy tartan material.

She poured out the tea in two cups and handed one to each of the brothers.

"Whatever would we do without you, Mrs. Kemper?" Clive said, bestowing a charming smile on her.

"Oh, Mr. Clive, you're too much for a poor old woman," she said with a girlish giggle and bustled out.

"Good lady, that," he said. "Better watch whom you marry and bring into the household. Mrs. Kemper wouldn't like her territory infiltrated," Clive, the practised troublemaker, said, watching her leave the room.

Gordon stood up. "I am retiring early tonight. Tomorrow I go to the neighbouring county to contract with a new buyer for the wool after sheep shearing season."

"All praise to you, brother. More business. You do our parents proud." Clive gave a dry laugh.

"You'd do well to learn the business and help me. Get up at the crack of dawn to supervise the hands each day," Gordon said, trying to keep his voice from tightening, and using every fibre in his being to appear patient.

He picked up the hat that lay on the floor and walked to the bellpull for Mrs. Kemper to take the tea service away.

Gordon called to the dogs and left the room.

After his brother's footsteps died away toward the east wing of the manor, Clive strode around the large drawing room admiring the solid oak panelling, the old but sturdy and comfortable rugs, the sofa and armchairs, the old spinet piano that his mother used to play when he and Gordy were little.

On the walls hung portraits of bygone ancestors, respectable gentry, who had live off the land. The poor blokes, who trudged out in plus fours and tweed jackets.

Clive let out a snort. "No gentleman farmer's life for me," he muttered to himself as he ran a finger lightly over the yellowed keys of the spinet. Life was replete with adventure and fortune for the taking. He had had his fill of back-break drudgery in the mines of

Africa. Now he wanted to enjoy freedom and the things that money could buy. And that included Viola.

What did they know of true hard work under an equatorial sun, sweat pouring down the face, the stench of the swamps when the tropical rains set in?

Clive inspected the paintings of his father and grandfather and his father before him. He felt neither kinship nor admiration as Gordy obviously felt. "More fool he," Clive muttered.

He turned toward the winding staircase outside the drawing room and went up to his room, the room he had known as a child.

Clive entered it and looked around. Its oak panel and rough-hewn furniture beckoned him as before, but now it engendered boredom within him. The feeling lay dull and heavy in his chest. He was back at his homestead but without a purpose to guide him.

He threw himself on the bed, boots and all. Tomorrow he would go to the smoking rooms of London, a few hours journey by train from East Brighton and see how the gentry passed its time in this anaemic society.

His hand went to his throat. He felt stifled, encumbered, as if entrenched in a straightjacket. If it hadn't been for Viola these many days… Yet his past life hung over his head like the sword of Damocles. He

103

had to keep it secret a while longer until he won fair Viola.

He sprang up suddenly and strode to the long window and pulled back the heavy tasseled curtain.

The moonlight lay like a swathe of silver on the grounds of Thornton Croft. The old, worn stone turrets rose like sentinels looming against a pale midnight sky and the sundial mounted on the stone pillar stood like a knight's sword waiting to fall on the approaching enemy.

This place seizes your soul, but I am an alien here after the white heat and blazing orange sunset skies of the trackless African desert, he thought, and turned away with a heavy sigh.

He had travelled in the Sahara and spent days wandering with the Bedouin, learning their ways, riding their camels and horses for days without water. He had ridden in Bedouin camel and horse races and had won the coveted prize for their tribal chieftain. They did not call him "Khamsin" for nothing, for he rode like the wind, the sirocco of the desert, a veritable daredevil on horseback.

On his return to Sussex, he had ridden his brother's horses, Jim and Caper, out onto the fields but it was nothing like the feeling he had had from conquering the desert on horseback. His name was known among the

"Bedu" for his fearlessness. Now he had returned to the life of a respectable landed gentry to hide away, and it tore into his soul.

A movement in the cold white light of the moon stopped his thoughts and he squinted into the distance. Somebody was there – a horse thief? His hand clutched the curtain for a second, then he let it fall from his grip in a single movement.

Who was it? He had to investigate, accost the intruder. He descended the staircase stealthily. The good Mrs. Kemper had retired for the evening and the workmen had all gone home after the day's labour.

He let himself out through the side door leading out of the kitchen onto the stone terrace and moved lightly toward the grounds with the stealth of a wily cat.

A figure darted between two trees, and Clive followed, closing the distance between himself and the man, for it was a man – tall and well built.

Clive pounced on him from behind. The man wore a cape of some kind. This Clive used to encircle his head as one would use a butterfly net.

The man fell to the ground and rolled free of Clive's grip. He rose and turned on Clive with almost superhuman force and pinioned him against a tree.

"Who are you and what do you want?" Clive said, almost choking in the visor-like grip of the man.

The moon slid into view from behind the clouds and the man's heavy, swarthy features became visible.

"Surely you remember me?" the man said.

"Van Kleer," Clive said, wheezing to take a breath. "What do you want?"

"My money. The money you were to invest for me in the diamond mining company, but which you gambled away," the man said in a guttural voice. "Where is it? I have come to claim it. Cough it up."

"How do you think I arrived here at my family's homestead? I am a wealthy man, my friend," Clive said with bravado, hoping the man was fooled. "Look around you. The lands, the livestock. My forebears and I are landowners. I am worth ten times the amount I borrowed from you."

"Then suppose you give it to me now. No. You gambled your inheritance away. A leopard does not change its spots. Gambling is in your blood and it's only a matter of time before you gamble away your property and your brother's livelihood." The man made a vigorous move and held his forearm against Clive's throat and pulverized him against the tree trunk. "If you don't give me the money, I go to the police, to your brother, whom you have probably duped into thinking you made a fortune at the Kimberley diamond mines, to your lady friend and the countless others you have fooled. Mark my words."

So, the man had been shadowing Clive for many days. How else could he have known about Viola?

Clive took a moment to answer. "Alright." He said in a hoarse whisper. "Give me room to breathe."

The man loosened his grip on Clive's throat with a jerk. "Start talking."

"Look Van Kleer. I'll make a bargain with you."

"You'll do no such thing. I make the decisions between you and me." He pushed Clive back against the tree trunk. "The money, or else."

"Alright. Calm yourself, my friend."

"I am not your friend. You will pay me tomorrow."

"I will need time to arrange to get it."

"Tomorrow night at the Boar's Head Pub at the village of Rottingdean. And bring the money," Van Kleer said.

With a swift turn, he moved away and was gone.

The night closed in around Clive and, at first, he thought he had had a bad dream. Then he felt his throat, now pulsating from Van Kleer's throttling grip and realised that the man who had nearly choked him had not been a wraith.

Cold fear sliced into Clive like an unseen knife as he turned toward the homestead. He entered the way he had come outside, through the side entrance.

The sound of footsteps reverberated from the upstairs landing. Then Gordon appeared. "Clive, what is it? I heard voices. Drago and Cinnabar growled and wanted to be let outside but I kept them leashed."

"Just a vagabond who had lost his way," Clive replied nonchalantly.

"The good Mrs. Kemper must not be disturbed. She needs her rest, poor lady," Gordon said. "I am going to bed. Goodnight."

Clive trudged upstairs and closed the door of his room. He had to think. What could he do to rid himself of the millstone that had appeared out of nowhere? Where could he find the money?

The next evening, Gordon disappeared on his rounds to the surrounding counties, "To inspect livestock to purchase," he told Clive. "I will be away a few days."

Just as well, Clive thought, as he dressed to leave and pulled on his galoshes for it had started to rain.

He told Mrs. Kemper that he was dining out and not to wait up, that he would let himself in on his return.

Clive managed to get into a compartment of the last train into the village of Rottingdean and settled in. The rain pelted the windowpane and the gloom outside deepened as the locomotive trundled along through the misty countryside.

When he reached the village, he set off on foot, a mile's walk to the Boar's Head Pub. He paused near some yew tress and waited, Through the undulating mist he saw the silhouette of a tall man walking toward the oak door of the pub. The man wore a cloak.

Clive moved ahead stealthily. He laid a hand on the man's shoulder.

"Van Kleer," Clive said. "It is I."

The man wheeled around. "So, you have come. Do you have the money?"

"Yes. Never fear. But first, how came you to be in England?"

"That is of no concern to you."

"Old times' sake, old boy," Clive said, affecting jocularity. He pointed to an old iron bench in the distance. "We can talk there. The pub is a busy place. I'm sure they have no place for two more."

"No. I have no time. I have hired a hansom cab to take me back to my hotel," Van Kleer said nodding in its direction. Then he looked at Clive. "The money. Let's have it."

Clive jerked his head toward the alley behind the pub. "I have hidden it there. If you will just walk with me a distance, it's yours." He waited for the man's response.

Van Kleer started walking.

The alley was dark, dank, and slick with rain. In a trice, Clive pinned Van Kleer, who was caught unawares, against the gray stone wall of the dingy building that housed the Boar's Head, and drove a knife into the man's chest. Van Kleer fell to the ground like a heavy, wet sack of peat moss.

* * * *

The inky blackness of the night cloaked Clive's movements until he reached Thornton Croft drenched in rain. He had taken the train back and walked the rest of the way in the pulsating downpour.

Not a soul stirred as he let himself in. Drago and Cinnabar, ever alert, approached him and sniffed suspiciously, then slinked away to continue their slumber on the old tartan blanket.

Clive went up the stairs. Only when he reached his room did he breathe freely. He had killed a man. He hadn't wanted to do it but the man would have surely ruined him.

A plan was forming in his mind. He would have to leave. Run for a while until things settled. A man would be found knifed in the alley behind the pub, but it could be attributed to a brawl.

110

He would have to make his move soon and Gordy would chalk it up to Clive's eternal wanderlust. Who was to know?

By the time Gordon returned, the news had spread with the efficiency of tom-tom drums dispersing news through the tribes of the Congo.

Gordon had barely hauled in his clothes bag, when he said, "A man was murdered near the Boar's Head, It was said that he was not from these parts."

Clive feigned disinterest. "They will apprehend the miscreant for sure."

"Well, I am home. My visit to the counties was a success." Gordon pulled off his boots and let them lie where they fell in the hallway.

"I take it you purchased livestock?" Clive said.

"A Hereford and a few sheep. The seller will bring them tomorrow."

They walked into the drawing room where Mrs. Kemper had lit the fireplace with the help of the stable boy.

Gordon peered at Clive. He had always been a little short sighted. "How have you been entertaining yourself? Has Viola been here?" This last was said with what appeared like trepidation.

"Calm yourself, brother. I have not seen Viola," Clive said, trying to sound flamboyant and confident as

111

usual. But now his feigning talents were starting to fail him. He wanted to be as far removed from Thornton Croft and from Sussex as possible. "I am leaving."

"Leaving?" Gordon's eyebrows lifted in surprise. "Why?"

"Wanderlust. I am going to Arabia to race thoroughbreds. Sheikh Kareem al Rasheed has invited me to compete at the Ocean of Fire horse race. I plan to take him up on the offer." He had just now thought of the plan. But he would convince Sheikh Rasheed to let him race one of his Arabian horses, the one Clive had helped the Sheikh select when he had come to Kimberley the year before to purchase diamonds.

"What is it? Money?" Gordon asked.

"Yes. And why not?"

"I thought you had enough and more," Gordon said.

"It is never enough. Or do you not care for money?"

"Have you pledged your word to Viola that you will marry her?" Gordon asked.

"No. I have not asked her to marry me yet." His attraction for Viola had been short-lived, transient. His own life was more important than Viola now. He could not stay here. "You are free to court her as I don't know when I will return." Or if I'll return, he thought.

Gordon gave him a piercing look. "What is the reason for this defection? For defection it is."

"Keep your noble thoughts to yourself. Enough that you are free to woo your fair Viola," Clive said.

The animosity between the brothers charged the room like electricity, but Gordon let his brother's remark pass for the moment. "Do as you please," Gordon said finally as he turned toward the stairs.

In the cold mist of the early morning, Gordon said farewell to Clive as Clive took a hansom cab to Southampton, and from there, a steamer to Calais.

Cold silence hung heavily in the air as Clive left. Neither man spoke beyond a terse "Goodbye."

Late that evening, Inspector Kettridge from Scotland Yard called on Gordon.

"Is something wrong," Gordon asked as Mrs. Kemper showed the inspector in.

"Good evening," Kettridge said, removing his hat. "I suppose you are aware that a man has been killed by an alley near the Boar's Head?"

"So I heard," Gordon replied.

"The man was from South Africa and a slip of paper was found in one of his pockets with your brother's name on it."

"Clive? How can that be? What would he have to do with this man?" Gordon said.

"Your brother has been away for several years. There may be a great many things you don't know about him," the inspector said.

Heaviness dragged Gordon down like a ton weight. Clive's sudden departure, his evasiveness, all attested to some guilt on his part. "How can you be sure my brother has anything to do with the murder?" Gordon said.

"The driver of the hansom cab the man came in was at a short distance from them and provided some description of what he saw in the available light. Our department has produced a drawing of the man." He showed Gordon a sketch. It was the picture of a tall man with curly hair and distinctive attire.

"This doesn't prove anything, Inspector," Gordon said. "I'm not convinced this is my brother."

"There's a pond nearby which our men are searching for the knife that was used to stab the victim," Kettridge said. "I must ask also that your brother remain here."

"My brother is not here. He left for Arabia, to participate in a horse race, he said."

The inspector made a sudden movement. "Not here? In that case, we must start extradition procedures to have him brought back to Britain."

"Do what you must, Inspector."

* * * *

The sun still blazed brightly while it dipped like a red balloon genuflecting against the pink sky in the distance. A cool breeze flapped the elaborate black-and-gold-threaded garments of sheikhs and attendants. The horses, tired from the race of several days, now reposed in their stables amidst the mud-brick ruins of the historic ancient city of Diriyyah, in the heart of the Arabian Peninsula, known as Najd.

Sheikh Kareem al Rasheed felicitated Clive on his victorious race, and celebrations were now underway.

"Name your price," the Sheikh said. "What would you like to be paid in? Money? Horses?"

The race had been won, but Clive felt no victory. And this had surprised him. The laurel that had spelled triumph had meant nothing to him. Here in the desert he could have stayed for a lifetime ruminating about his past life. He loved the desert as nothing else. This surprised him too. He had sought money for gambling all his life, but now it seemed pallid.

The night before the race, he had received a letter from his brother. "Clive," he wrote. "You are a wanted man here. The man who was killed – Scotland Yard thinks you had something to do with it. You know

115

beyond words that I would stand by you, but you must live with yourself. Do what you think is best. Ever yours, Gordon."

The note had saddened him. His brother was a better man than he, Clive, could ever be.

Clive looked at the Sheikh. He knew what he must do now. "I want no price," he said. "I rode in the race because it was a journey I had to make to find myself. Now I must return to England."

"And have you found yourself?"

"Yes. I believe I have."

"In that case, go, my friend," the Sheikh said. "And may Allah go with you. You have brought honour to my tribe by winning the Ocean of Fire race. Uphold that honour like a beacon. It will guide you."

* * * *

Gordon was waiting when Clive returned to Thornton Croft many days later. The fireplace had been lit as before, and Drago and Cinnabar greeted him as if they saw him as a hero. They could never know what he had done in his previous life. Or could they?

"I am home to pay my debts," Clive said to Gordon. As he went inside, he saw another man.

"This is Inspector Kettridge from Scotland Yard,"

116

Gordon said.

The man rose and walked toward Clive.

8

THE FILM FESTIVAL

BY EMMA SALKILD

I check my watch as the train departs Central Station. It's 6:45am and I've been up for nearly three hours because I needed to put my hair in curlers for a Grace Kelly do. I copied her character Margot Wendice from the 1954 Hitchcock film: *Dial M for Murder*.

Besides a few filmy types, the train I'm on is dead empty, so I decide to snooze. After about twenty minutes of dozing I pull out my laptop and start typing. A man, probably in his forties, gets on the train and sits in the aisle across from me. He's slightly overweight and wearing a suit.

'Excuse me sir,' I say, 'but what is that strange parcel you have on the luggage rack above you?'

'Oh,' he says, 'that's a Macguffin.'

'Well,' I say, 'what's a Macguffin?'

'It's an apparatus for trapping lions in Huskisson.'

118

'But,' I say, 'there are no lions in Huskisson.'

'Well,' he says, 'then that's no Macguffin.'

We both laugh at this Hitchcockian reference. Although when the film god used the quote it wasn't Huskisson but the Scottish Highlands.

'What are you typing?' he asks me.

'Oh,' I say, 'I always type in Courier New because it's the screenplay font. If I could, I would speak in Courier New.'

'I meant what are you writing about?'

'Oh, a few films I watched last night. I'm a film-criticism student and the main journalist for the campus newspaper.'

'Sounds interesting. Can I have a read sometime?'

'Sure.'

'Well, you keep plugging away and you can show me over dinner tonight if you like. I assume you're on your way to the film festival too.'

'I sure am. Dinner would be great.' I keep typing but it's in gobbledygook because I'm thinking about the 1951 Hitchcock film, Strangers on a Train, where a man was falsely accused of killing his wife. I notice the man on the train is reading a novel and I wonder if it's by Patricia Highsmith because Hitchcock had based films on her books.

My phone beeps and it's a message from Lisa, "my

assistant". My editor, Mark, hired her. Protesting didn't get me anywhere. Ugh. She's a med student with a psychology minor and knows nothing about film. I think she wants to be a psychiatrist. It's silly that she even got a job as my assistant. Mark and Lisa had insisted she drive me down to Huskisson for the film festival too. Can you imagine? She can be quite controlling. It's as though she works for some cabal where she has to get me to do it 'her way' all the time. So yesterday, I did a no-show and she got so worried that she drove down thinking I had already made my way there. Now she knows I'm on the train, she's insisting on picking me up from the station in Nowra. She's there already so I don't know how I'm going to avoid her.

It was very important I caught the train on my own. Anything can happen this way. So many films have train scenes and I wanted to acquaint myself with it. Also, I find trains very, very sexy. I look over to my stranger. With that suit, and slightly bigger frame he really is quite attractive, in a Hitchcockian type of way. Maybe I can take advantage of the lift from Lisa.

'Excuse me,' I say to him. 'I was just wondering if you would like a lift from Nowra to Huskisson.'

'Thanks,' he says, 'but I'm already getting picked up.'

120

'Oh, by whom?' I ask. He raises an eyebrow. Whoops, was that too blunt?

'By Ruth Walker.'

'The festival co-ordinator? You know her?'

'Yes, I do,' he says. 'She's my wife. So you never told me your name.'

'Patricia,' I say, 'Patricia Hayes.'

'Tony Walker. And I hope you can still make dinner tonight. I'd like to read your writing.'

He hands me a piece of paper with Anthony Walker written on it and his phone number. I hesitate for a moment so as not to appear too keen, and then I take the paper, fold it and put in it my bra. This makes him laugh.

'Sounds delightful,' I say. 'I'll ring you once I'm settled.' I give him a smile and walk over to my seat. The train starts to slow, and I glance out the window. There are green paddocks with dairy cows. Who would have thought? What a fascinating location for a film festival. I grab my portmanteau, and I can see Lisa waiting on the platform. Her hair is short and burgundy. She wears dark (almost gothic) make up, baggy jeans and a cardigan. It frustrates me I can't pinpoint what style she is. One thing's for sure, she's definitely not Hitchcock. I give her the up-and-down. She's not Tarentino, Lucas, Spielberg, Kubrick, Allen, Fellini,

Scorcese, Luhrman, Stone, Cohen, Jackson, Bergman, Coppola, Cassavetes, Scott, Lee, Polanski, Lynch or Burton. Well, maybe Tim Burton. I could be on to something with that one.

I step on to the platform and Lisa waves at me.

'You look great,' she says.

'Thanks.'

Tony passes me and gives me a wink, before getting into a car. Sitting in the driver's seat is a stylish-looking brunette woman, whom he kisses on the cheek.

'Car's this way,' Lisa says, but I'm standing frozen, my eyes glued to Tony and Ruth until the car drives away and I can no longer see them.

We get into her Magna. It's clean and smells like those small pine tree cut-outs, but I can't see one anywhere. She puts on some rock music which I turn down. I notice that she keeps watching me, scanning me over as though taking mental notes.

'What is it?' I ask.

'Huh? Oh, your hair. It's great.'

'Thanks. I was channelling Margot Wendice.'

'Who?' she asks me. I scowl at her ignorance, and then remember about Burton.

'Oh,' I say, 'that reminds me, are you Burton?'

'Burton what?'

'Tim Burton? Is that your scene? I was him for

about ten days. I've switched between a few directors but I've never been as happy as I am with Hitchcock. The man is a genius.'

'Was, you mean, he was a genius. He's dead,' she says. I shift uncomfortably in my seat.

'You're very Helen Bonham Carter,' I say. 'Especially when she was in Sweeney Todd or Big Fish. Or maybe you're Winona Ryder too, but in *Beetlejuice*, not in *Edward Scissorhands*. You're not blonde enough for that.'

Lisa looks at me with her mouth open and squinty eyes. Poor thing. She seems to have a low self-esteem.

'Don't worry,' I say, 'Winona could only just pull that one off.'

'How do you know that man? The one at the train station?' she asks.

'Who? Oh him. Just someone I met on the train. He's another Hitchcock appreciator.'

Lisa raises an eyebrow, 'really?'

'It's actually none of your business.'

'You're right, I'm sorry,' she says with insincerity oozing from her pores. She is definitely Helen Bonham Carter today. Shifty, like Marla in Fincher's Fight Club.

We pull into Huskisson. The air is warm and the blue waters sparkle and shine like something from a

123

Spielberg film. There's a hum of chatter and laughs. The streets are lined with information tables, people in festival shirts, and food stalls. Huskisson has been completely overrun by all the Sydney film people. It's brilliant.

'Let's get a program,' I say to Lisa, and we walk over to the cinema where they will be screening the films. The theatre is gorgeous. It's small and quaint and painted a coral pink and green to match its sea milieu. I take a program and start to circle all the films I want to see. As I look up I see Joel Edgerton and Alex Dimitriades walk in to a coffee shop. They're in ripped jeans and t-shirts with unshaven faces and unwashed hair. They were probably channelling Johnny Depp, and that look wouldn't mesh with mine. All the same, I would like to get a closer look.

'Thanks so much for picking me up Lisa,' I say.

'My pleasure,' she says.

'Let me buy you a coffee.'

Her eyes brighten, 'I would love that.'

We go into the coffee shop. It's more of a café/fruit and veggie shop that sells expensive gourmet sauces and jams. We sit down at the table next to Joel. It turns out he's not with Alex after all because they're sitting at different tables.

'Huskisson has a "no plastic" policy,' Lisa says,

'it's quite amazing. All the customers bring cardboard boxes and paper bags. There's not a single plastic bag in the whole place.'

'Why? What's the point?'

'To be environmentally friendly.'

'What about cling wrap then? Have they banned that too?'

I pull out my laptop.

'Lisa, as my assistant, would you please read out this article I wrote?' I ask. 'I want to hear what it sounds like.'

Lisa looks around at all the people in the café. 'What here? Now?' she asks.

'Yes, please. That would be grand,' I say.

She breathes in, pulls the laptop towards her and begins to read aloud. I slyly look to Joel and Alex to see if they overhear.

'Proud feminist and blonde-bombshell, Patricia Hayes, reviews the timelessness, fascination and underlying danger in the sub-genre of Hollywood femme fatale, psychological thrillers.

What do the films *Basic Instinct*, *Fatal Attraction* and more recently *Basic Instinct 2* have in common? I'm not only referring to the hyper-sexualised deadly blonde leads of Sharon Stone and Glenn Close. The films create a fear, in both genders, of power-hungry, successful womyn. The deadly-womyn characters Catherine Tramell (*Basic Instinct*) and Alex Forrest (*Fatal Attraction*) are beautiful, rich and successful in their careers. Tramell is a famous novelist and Forrest is an intelligent publishing editor. The screenplays, which were both written by men, James Dearden (*Fatal Attraction*) and Joe Eszterhas (*Basic Instinct*), also share another similarity; the lead womyn are out to ruin men. Both protagonists are played by Michael Douglas and the characters are Dan Gallagher (*Fatal Attraction*) and Nick Curran, nickname Shooter (*Basic Instinct 1*). Gallagher and Curran are portrayed as having faults and making mistakes but in the end they are all-round good blokes. But whoopsie, all of a sudden, a successful and beautiful womyn comes along and causes havoc for the good guys. They aim to destroy careers, ruin current love lives or any potential of future ones and will be sure to kill a few innocents along the way (animals included).'

Lisa looks up from the laptop.

'Why did you write this Patricia?' she asks.

'For the uni paper.'

'But why this story?' she looks around the room nervously, and then turns back to me. 'Don't you think it's odd that you watch these particular films and then you try to see a married man?'

I look at Lisa suspiciously. Is she fishing for something?

'I don't know what you're talking about,' I say. I look over at Joel, hoping he's not listening to Lisa's rant and thankfully he's not. Alex is staring at me, although I think it's safe. He doesn't appear to be listening to the conversation, but rather checking out my legs.

'I love it when men look at my legs,' I say trying to change the subject. 'I remember the first time I was checked out. I was wolf-whistled by a group of men passing by in a car. I was twelve years old and in cut-off denim shorts, walking to my friend's house.'

'What are you talking about? Look Patricia, Mark and I are worried about you. I mean, this article, doesn't even sound like you. Sometimes you write feminist criticism and then other times, you plan affairs and go on about how men ogle you.'

'This is ridiculous.'

'I'm just saying you change all the time by switching personalities. It's not healthy.'

I stand up slowly and place a twenty-dollar note on the table.

'Thank you for the lift Lisa, but I'm going to find the motel and freshen up and I will call you later.'

'Come on Pat,' she says. 'Don't make a drama out of this. We need to talk about it.'

'Number one, I'm not Pat but Patricia. And number two, drama is life with the dull bits left out, which is why I'm walking away from you.'

I turn around feeling very proud of myself. I had taken Hitch's quote "drama is life with the dull bits left out" to a whole new level. My body tingles with the adrenalin, but I still manage to exit the premises with style and grace.

As soon as I leave the café I ring Tony.

'Hi Mr. Walker, this is Patricia Hayes from the train. What are you doing now? I've got to see you. My room number is 302. I'm staying at the Dolphin Motel.'

I'm aware of my heart racing wildly in my chest. Everything else around me has come to a standstill.

'That would be delightful,' he says.

I want to yell, 'yippee'.

'See you then,' I say as I hang up the phone and casually walk to the motel. I chortle when I see the place. It's dark blue with green starfish painted on it with a massive, plastic dolphin sitting over the entrance. The middle-aged woman checks me in and even shows me to my room. She chats happily away about the various sightseeing activities I can do. Scuba diving, kite surfing, whale cruises and so on. Her manner makes me feel welcome, but there is no way I'm getting my hair wet. It's funny she would even think for a second I'm that kind of a girl. I wish her a fond farewell and then lock the door.

My temporary boudoir has peach-coloured walls with photographs of penguins and whales. I collapse on to the bed and curl into a ball, but in a way that won't make my hair flat. My exhaustion surprises me. The day has taken its toll. I wonder where Lisa is and if I offended her. She's a strange one, but maybe I shouldn't have been so rude. I have to admit that it was kind of her to pick me up and she does seem to take an interest in me and what I do. There's a knock on the door. I take a deep breath in and pat down my hair and my skirt.

'Well, hello,' Tony says as I open the door. He presents me with a fruit basket.

'How quaint,' I say as I take the basket from him. 'Would you like a piece? I can't really offer you anything else.'

'Sure,' he says as he takes an orange. He bites into the peel and spits the chunk back into his hand, and then proceeds to peel it. I would never have chosen the orange. It's such a messy fruit with a potent smell, but as I watch him pull the skin off it, I see that this was the perfect fruit to be eating for a situation like this. He passes me a chunk of three pieces together and I try to daintily pull off a piece but some juice squirts on to my cheek. I wipe it off, giggling, and he laughs too. His laughter is warm and jovial and makes me feel as though I'm being wrapped up in a blanket. I lie down on the bed, and pull him down with me. He leans over and kisses me with his citrus, zingy lips which makes my heart race again.

'You're beautiful,' he says.

'Thanks. Do you like blondes? I notice your wife is a brunette.'

He kisses me again, and then whispers into my ear, 'Blondes make the best victims. They're like virgin snow that shows up the bloody footprints.'

'I love that Hitch quote,' I say to him.

'I love how you refer to Hitchcock as Hitch.'

'You should use that quote when we next meet,' I say.

'Okay, my darling,' he says as he begins to kiss my neck.

'Our Macguffin line worked splendidly on the train this morning,' I say, but he's not really listening because his lips are finding their way down my neck to my chest.

'Let's practice the blonde line for our next

meeting,' I say as I pull away. A flash of disappointment spreads across his face.

'Okay, sure,' he says, and he grabs me by the waist, and nibbles on my ear. 'Blondes make the best victims. They're like virgin snow that shows up the bloody footprints.'

'No we have to practice it properly,' I say, 'like how we practiced the Macguffin line in my apartment that time.'

I stroke his hair, just the way he likes it.

'We could meet at the cinema,' I say, 'and see a film, and then go for dinner. I'll pretend I'm waiting for the film to begin.'

I get up and stand in the corner as though I'm waiting in a queue. Tony comes up behind me.

'Hello Miss, are you seeing this film alone?'

'Why, yes, would you care to join me?'

'I would,' he says as he presses his body close to mine. 'You're very beautiful.'

'Thanks. Do you like blondes?' I ask.

He pushes aside some of my hair and begins to kiss my neck, 'blondes make the best victims. They're like virgin snow that shows up the bloody footprints.'

I lift my neck to him so he can kiss it. He knows what turns me on. His lips are so smooth and soft on my neck. The soft lips start to trail down to my chest, his tongue wrapping around my bra, when his mobile rings. He pushes me away and answers.

'Hi, Ruth dear,' he says. 'I'll be there in ten. I just went wandering.'

I throw up my hands in disgust and he mouths "I'm sorry" to me before hanging up the phone.

'I have to run,' he says to me. I put my hands on my hips and pout.

'No, Tony, this is not acceptable,' I say, but he goes for the door. I block his way, and direct him to the bed so he falls back on it. I straddle him and stare down at his laughing eyes. I can see how much he enjoys being with me. I'm so sick of Ruth Walker getting in the way.

'I'm quite sure Ruth is busy with her film preparations tonight,' he says as he starts to unzip my dress. 'She really has been such a bore, you know. She goes on and on all the time about my direction.'

'But you're a wonderful reviewer,' I say as I unbutton his shirt. 'She is such a meany. I wish she would just disappear and leave us together forever. Then we could just watch films, and write about La Cinema.'

'As do I my dear,' he says, as he completely undresses me, and stares up at my body. 'Tonight will be fantastic,' he says as he starts to kiss me again. 'I'll get her out of our hair for good.'

Lisa isn't in her room, and hasn't left a message with the lady at reception. I call her for the third time but it rings out again. My arms have goose bumps that won't go away, and I pace the hallway of the motel, and then walk briskly out the door. I walk towards the coffee shop where I left her, but on the way I spot the burgundy hair in the Husky pub courtyard. The courtyard is large and inviting, although the pub itself is verging on tacky with Husky pub souvenirs for sale. The front part of the pub is full of smiling, bearded locals and women in out-of-fashion high heels who play pool and have warm, happy laughs. The back part of the pub is more family-orientated with video games in the corner and a large kitchen with lots of fish and seafood. Outside there are long, wooden benches on soft, healthy grass, overlooking the bay and boats.

Lisa is on the phone and appears to be wrapped in a serious conversation, her face twisted into a grimace. I haven't seen her with such an expression before. As I walk up to her, she spots me coming and puts on a warm smile and waves.

'Look Lisa,' I say as I sit down next to her, 'I just want to apologise about my outburst earlier today. You can call me Pat. No one has called me that before. It's

133

kind of sweet.'

'It's okay,' she says. 'Apology accepted. I'm just glad you're alright.'

She rubs my arm and gives me such a lovely smile that for some reason tears are in my eyes and rolling down my face.

'Are you okay?' she asks. 'What is it, Pat?'

'Oh nothing,' I say, 'I get so emotional after making love sometimes. Silly really, and I felt bad for getting angry at you. Then I couldn't find you and you weren't answering your phone.'

'You just had sex?' she asks. I raise a hand to my mouth.

'Um …'

'Look Pat, you can tell me.' Her eyes are so wide, yet so soft and strangely beautiful. I want to tell her about Tony and Ruth, and all our games, just so I can share it with someone. But then I worry that it wouldn't be as special. If I blabbed then maybe my encounters with Tony would become less private, and less intimate. The excitement might dwindle and disappear.

'It's nothing.' I say.

'Is it Tony?' she asks me. I'm about to answer 'yes' when it dawns on me, how would she know about Tony? I haven't told anyone about him. Those eyes are staring into mine, trying to soothe me.

'Pat, Pat,' she says, as she tugs on my hand, 'are you okay?'

I feel so tired, like I could sleep forever, but I want to see Tony again today, and to feel his arms around me as we whisper sweet Hitchcock-nothings to each other.

'Yeah, I'm fine. I'm going to a film tonight.'

'Great, can I come?' she asks.

'No.'

'Look, let me get you a drink,' she says. I nod and watch her enter the pub and go around the corner into the bar. I decide that this would be the best time to do a runner. I start to walk past the bar when I see something unusual. Lisa is with a tall, ginger-haired cop. The two are whispering into each other's ear. I see her point out to the back to where we were just sitting. I'm about to turn around, when she notices me. Her face drops and the policeman, whose back has been to me, turns around and looks at me. Lisa swallows, looks nervously to the policeman, and then picks up the drinks and comes over to me. The policeman quickly walks away.

'Sorry I took so long,' she says as she hands me a tumbler glass of ice and a clear liquid which could be gin or vodka. I scan her face, trying to work out what was going on.

'Who was that?'

'Who? Oh, the cop? Um, he was just waiting for a

135

drink at the bar too.' She says. I continue to stare.

'A drink?' I ask.

'Of water, of course. Yes, he was waiting for a drink of water. Let's go outside.'

She leads me to a table in the courtyard and I sit down and take a sip of my drink. It tastes strong, and I remember I haven't eaten. I don't want to get tipsy, but I drink it anyway. Lisa is fidgeting, when something catches her eye.

'Excuse me,' she says as she quickly leaves the table. I'm getting a bit tired of her nonsense and I finish my drink and aim for another escape. Until I spot Lisa with Ruth, Tony's wife. Lisa is talking animatedly to Ruth with occasional glances towards me. I make my way over, paranoid that she might say something about Tony.

'Look Lisa,' I hear Ruth say, 'I have an important meeting to go to now and you are in my way.'

On my approach, the two women go quiet.

'Ms Walker, how are you?' I say.

'Why, Patricia Hayes. I'm well, thank you,' she says to me. 'How's all the writing going?'

'Great thank you. I noticed you didn't accept my latest film review for your magazine,' I say.

'Yes, well, sorry about that,' she says smirking.

'Okay, Lisa and I must be off. I have a film to

catch.'

'Which one? I love to know which films people attend at my festival.'

'It's the six o'clock film,' Lisa says.

Ruth's eyes go wide. 'Tony is seeing that film,' she says.

'Who?' I ask.

'My husband,' she says, 'and if I remember correctly you two hit if off at the last film festival I organised.'

'Oh yes, yes,' I say, 'he was interesting. Well we might see him there. Come on Lisa,' I say taking her arm. I don't want them talking to each other.

'I think I might join you,' Ruth says.

'Don't you have a meeting?' Lisa asks.

Ruth shrugs.

'That would be lovely Ms Walker,' Lisa says.

As the three of us walk down the main drag, I picture my Tony standing in the foyer, and how we were going to play-act strangers, and recite the Hitchcock lines to each other. Lisa is the one to blame for all this mess. I feel like slapping her for all the trouble she has caused, but I couldn't actually slap Lisa. There is something about her that is growing on me. Maybe it's her intensity, her warmth, and something quite mysterious. She's up to something and I feel as though she may become a Hitchcock groupie too. She might even be like Barbara Morton in Strangers on a Train, whose character was played by Hitchcock's daughter, Patricia. A connection such as that should not to be taken lightly. I shiver with excitement as I watch Lisa try to make eye contact with Ruth. It's as though she's trying to tell her a story without me noticing. It's not working because Ruth has her eyes on me. They look as though they could glow red, like a woman possessed. Ruth's grimace slyly transforms into a plastered smile. The pearls around her neck twinkle and dazzle as she curls them around her long, painted fingers. I picture my own painted nails on those pearls, caressing them and feeling them fall between my fingers before I tighten them around her pale neck until they work as a harness, cutting off her air.

'Ruth,' I hear a man's voice say, breaking my daydream. Tony is standing there next to Ruth. My stranger with my enemy.

'Tony, I ran into Patricia. You remember her from the Moon Tide Festival in Newtown.'

'Oh yes of course, how are you,' he says and his warm sweaty hand is thrust into mine.

'Hi,' I say and give an award-winning smile while I try to bat my eyelashes. I'm not going to hold back tonight and that cow Ruth can just suffer and choke.

'This is Lisa, Patricia's friend,' Ruth says. Tony extends his hand to Lisa, and she looks at it suspiciously. He turns to me as if looking for answers but I just continue to smile. Finally, Lisa shakes his hand, her face stern and uncompromising.

After the film, Tony suggests we all go to the fair. I nod in agreement. Ruth and Lisa are silent, eyes darting from person to person. I'm desperate for Tony and me to recite our Hitchcock lines and the fair would be a good opportunity. Sitting through the film had been torture, but that exciting torture that occurs when you are forced to wait, and wait, and wait. It's sort of like watching a Hitchcock film. Throughout the movie I had been next to Lisa, who was next to Ruth, who was next to Tony. The two women had managed to get me three seats away from him but now the four of us are walking to the fair, and I've managed to get on his right hand side.

It's a dark and balmy night and suspense is in the air. The fair is small but busy. There are crowds of teenage boys in skinny leg jeans and side-swept fringes who clutch skateboards. They look over to girls in denim miniskirts or cargo shorts who try to look mature by speaking on mobile phones or smoking cigarettes. The sounds of laughter and screams mingle together and are heard over the distant crashes of the ocean. There are dodgem cars, a Ferris wheel, a big slide, flying chairs, a round up and a cha cha. The filmy types look happy, and are taking turns at shooting plastic ducks, or popping balls down the throats of moving, guffawing clowns.

Lisa excuses herself, and I'm left with Ruth and Tony.

'Who wants to go on the flying chairs with me?' he asks.

'You know I hate heights,' Ruth says.

'Patricia?' he asks me. I'm not keen on the flying chairs and heights either, but I say yes, wanting to make the most of an opportunity alone with Tony. Ruth raises a hand in protest, when her mobile phone rings. Tony gives her a quick kiss on the cheek and then quickly leads me away to the flying chairs. We wait in the queue together. There's a small boy and girl in front of us, around the age of eight. The boy is shoving fairy floss into his mouth and refusing to share with the girl.

'Say the line,' I whisper to Tony.

'Don't be stupid,' he says. His face is hard and cold and I take a step backwards.

'Tony? What's the matter with you?' I ask. He grabs my wrist.

'Just shut up,' he says. 'Who's that girl, Lisa?'

'My assistant,' I say. His grip gets tighter.

'Yeah, well I don't trust her. I had plans for tonight and she's ruining them.'

My wrist starts to throb and I try to twist it out of his grasp.

'Hurry up,' a voice says behind me. Tony and I are pushed onto chairs and he sits in front of me, and the fairy floss boy and girl are in front of Tony. The back of Tony's neck looks strong and masculine. I reach out but I'm too far away and I can't touch him. I wish we had our night together like we planned and I try to edge towards him but then the chair begins to move on its own. The ride has begun. I place my feet on the grass so I'm walking with the chair, and trying to catch up to Tony. The speed picks up as the chair starts to lift. The wind blows out my hair and I feel incredible, as though I'm a little kid again. I throw back my head and laugh up at the Huskisson stars. When I look at Tony, he is still staring straight ahead. I want him to turn to me, to smile at me, wink at me, anything, but I know he's thinking about Ruth. Anger rushes over me and I want to get off the chair and find Ruth. I want her out of my life.

I hear a heaving sound, followed by a scream of "ewww". The kid in front of Tony is vomiting up his fairy floss. It falls like a sprinkler down on the grass

141

below. Bile rises up in my stomach and I turn away in disgust and try to focus on anything but the child. Something catches my eye. Ruth and Lisa are standing on the outskirts of the fair and behind them is dense, dark bush. They look like they are yelling at each other. I pass the women as the chairs go around, and I turn my head to get a better look but the pole in the middle of the ride is obscuring them. Finally, I get back round to where they are standing and I see Lisa grab Ruth by the arms and shake her. Ruth seems to be crying. Then Lisa slaps her, hard. Ruth runs off into the bush and is followed by Lisa. I lose sight of them again and I look in front of me, waiting for the ride to get back to where I last saw them. Tony has been watching too with clenched fists. The kid continues to vomit and the smell becomes stronger. When the ride stops I unbuckle my strap and collapse on the grass and pull back my hair before a large amount of vomit tumbles out of my mouth. I can hear others being sick around me and I wonder how Tony is, but I can't look up because I keep retching. Tears sting my eyes. I feel a man's hand on my back, and I'm so grateful that Tony has stopped to take care of me.

'Miss,' a voice says. 'The next ride needs to start.'

To my disappointment, the man peering down at me is the ride operator and not Tony. I look over to the bushy area and I can see the outline of a man disappearing into it.

'Are you okay, Miss?' the man asks me.

'Yeah, yeah, I have to get into the bush,' I reply as I get to my feet. There's a vomit taste in my mouth, and my eyes are stinging. I quickly wipe them and try to see clearly.

I stand at the edge of the bush and peer into it. It's dark and spooky and I can't see any shadows of the people in there. I look at my watch. It's 9:05pm. The fair is going to close in an hour and I still hadn't had the chance for Tony to approach me in a queue to say the Hitch quote. When I enter the bush I look to the ground for a path but there are only shrubs and twigs. I try to block out the sounds from the fair so that I can tune into what's going on around me. I walk further into the bush and a branch scrapes my arm, causing me to yell out in pain. My arm starts to bleed and I put a hand on it to stop the bleeding and it smears the blood across my forearm and through my fingers. I look around the dark, dense depths of the bush, and try to come up with a plan of action. I'm not sure if I should scream out for Tony or employ more stealth and try and find him so the others don't know we're together. Slowly, I walk further into the bush waiting for my eyes to adjust to the darkness. I think of Lisa and Ruth, and what could

143

have happened between them. Perhaps Lisa had slapped Ruth because she said nasty things about me. I feel worried about Lisa. It's a shame that Tony doesn't like her, but I felt the same way when I first met her. At first you think there is something odd about her, as though she is up to something. Then you get to know the real Lisa and she is down-to-earth and warm. My thoughts turn to Ruth and what a useless and pathetic woman she is. I move ahead with two thoughts crossing my mind: to find Tony; and to make sure Ruth will never be in our lives again.

I spend an hour in the bush searching for Tony and then decide to check the flying chairs in the hope that he is waiting for me there. As I walk out from the bush I see there are only a few stragglers hanging around and all the rides have been turned off. However, waiting by the flying chairs is a policemen talking to the ride operator. It is the tall, ginger-haired cop who Lisa had been talking with at the Husky pub.

'She's the one,' the ride operator says pointing to me. 'After her ride, she said she was going into the bush.'

'Are you Patricia Hayes?' he asks me as he looks down at my bloodstained arm.

'Yes,' I say.

'You're under arrest for the murder of Ruth Walker.'

I look up at the policeman, and nod in compliance.

The drive to the police station takes about six minutes from the fair. The Huskisson cop shop is tiny, and it's cute that they only have one person on duty tonight. The holding cell is adorable. I decide to pace, wringing my hands (because that's what they seem to do in the movies). It works well because my hands are shaking with excitement. I can't decide what to do, or who I want to be, or who I currently am. Would it be better to be the murderer? The victim? The accused?

I guess the small-town country nature is instilled in the police because the ginger-haired cop, Fred, gets me a cup of tea and pulls a chair up to the cell.

'Is there anything you want to say to me?' he asks.

'If this is what it's like being part of a Hitchcock film I might change directors. Perhaps Woody Allen would be better: light, neurotic and colourful.' I laugh at my joke.

'You do realise how serious this is?'

'Do you know any women who have been murderers in Hitchcock films? That's your first clue.'

He looks to the floor, and I see a sort of sorrow in his eyes.

145

'Psycho.'

'Excuse me,' I say.

'Norman Bates' mother, she was the murderer.'

'Yes, but that was a thriller/horror film. We're in a murder mystery.'

'Lisa was right about you,' he says.

'Where is she? What's happened to my Tony?' I ask. A shadow passes over his face.

'Lisa is missing, and Tony was the one who dobbed you in. He called us saying he saw you and Ruth go in to the bush. He said he couldn't find you and that he was worried because you had been acting strangely around him lately. He said he then heard a scream and that's when he rang us.'

Fred opens a notebook and flips a few pages open. 'This is his quote, "it's as though Patricia is one of the femme fatales in *Basic Instinct* or *Fatal Attraction*".'

I start to laugh, 'you can see why the two of us get along so well.'

'There are witnesses from the Husky coffee shop that heard you read an article about how you want to be a serial killer like Sharon Stone in *Basic Instinct*.'

My face drops. Either this is very bad luck, or very Hitchcock, or I really am the killer.

'But, I don't want to be Sharon Stone,' I say. 'I wanted to be Grace Kelly. I wanted to be the beautiful

146

blonde who lives in an exciting murder mystery. You know, "drama is life with the dull bits left out".'

'Patricia, I've got to give it to you. You're far from dull.'

'That's the sweetest thing I've heard all day.'

The cell is cold, and I'm brought extra blankets and dinner. It's not too bad. The cops are cheerful enough, the food is okay, and I could be in a worse position. Various films play over in my mind. If I stick to Hitchcock, I should be let off. The innocent are acquitted in the end in his films. If I'm the actual murderer, however, who knows what could happen. If I'm not guilty that leaves only Lisa or Tony? If it's Lisa, it's possible that Fred could be in on it. Then Tony would have to save me. If it's Tony, then Lisa or Fred will have to save me. I mean that's generally how the triangle happens. The ones who saved the falsely accused in *Dial M for Murder* and *Strangers on a Train* were the illicit lover and the cluey cops. Which makes me think, who would I prefer to rescue me? Tony or Lisa? I look around the cell. I've been incarcerated for hours. My face needs a wash. If only I had my computer so I could type something.

I hear a woman's voice and I recognise it as Lisa's. My stomach turns and my head starts to spin. I sit on the floor and wait for the dizzy spell to stop.

'Lisa,' Fred says, 'you're okay. Thank god, thank god.'

So Fred and Lisa are in this together. I inch as close to them as possible so I can hear better.

'He tried to kill me,' Lisa says in between gasps of air. She must have run here. I'm impressed.

'You've got to go find him,' she says. 'Now.'

'Who? Tony?'

'Yes,' Lisa says, 'He wanted us all dead.'

I hear Fred on the phone straightaway, calling cops to locate Tony.

'I have to see her Freddie, please,' she says.

Fred speaks in a hushed tone, 'I don't think that's a good idea.'

'You don't understand,' she says to him. 'She's not well.'

'You don't say. She thinks she's in a bloody Hitchcock film. Totally bonkers. I still think she might have done it. Maybe they're in it together.'

'She would never do this. It was Tony. I had been trying to talk to Ruth about their affair. I knew something was wrong. Then Ruth ran off into the bush. I followed her, and it took me ages to find her. When I did she was sitting on a log crying. I tried to comfort her when I felt a thick branch come down hard on my head. I collapsed to the ground and then saw Tony standing over Ruth. She ran off and Tony followed her. I managed to crawl away and find a rocky ledge. I climbed right under it hoping he wouldn't find me. Then I must have passed out. You've got to believe me Fred. It wasn't Patricia. No way.'

'Patricia is psychologically unstable. Tony said he was having an affair with her, and that she was extremely jealous of his wife.'

'She wouldn't kill someone. I know it. She wouldn't.'

Lisa starts to cry now. Her sobs are so unmovie-like, not to mention unladylike. The phone rings and Fred answers it.

'Lisa, he's split. Tony has left town. He checked out and bailed. This is bad. I've got to make phone calls. I'm sorry I can't talk right now.'

Fred starts to dial madly and Lisa walks up to my cell. She has cuts and scratches on her face.

'Are you okay, Pat?' Lisa asks. I nod my head and try to speak but it's hard to get the words out.

'You must be so scared, but you're safe now.'

'I'm not.'

'You are safe, I promise.'

'I mean I'm not scared.'

I walk to the other side of the cell and sit down.

149

'Pat, I was hired by Mark to watch you,' she says.

I turn back to her, 'what do you mean?'

'He was worried about you, because you seem so obsessed with films and directors and actors. Then he worked out when you started seeing Tony. He got very concerned about how this would impact on you. He wanted me to keep an eye on you to make sure you were okay.'

My temples start to throb, and I raise a tremulous hand to my head.

'I feel very strange Lisa.'

'I'm studying to be a psychiatrist. Mark thinks you need professional help and after assessing you over the past few days, I do too. I knew you wouldn't be a danger to anyone else, but maybe to yourself. I warned Ruth about you and your health problems. I told her that she had to make sure you weren't around any men, including her husband, but she kept refusing to listen. I told her about the affair but she was in some sort of denial. Tony must have worked it out and took advantage of it to set you up.'

I walk to the farthest corner and crouch down with my hands over my ears.

'I think you're suffering from mild delusions, but without violent tendencies,' she says.

I burst out laughing, 'You're hilarious Lisa.'

'We're going to get you out of here, and into good care.'

Things don't seem so funny now, and for the first time since the arrest, my heart starts to beat very fast.

'I can't think of a film where the heroine suffers from a psychosis,' I say to her.

'What about *Vertigo*?' she asks.

'You watched *Vertigo*? But I didn't think you were into Hitchcock?'

'I hired a few Hitchcock films. I wanted to be able to talk to you about them.'

My mouth drops and tears start to fall down my face. That must be the second sweetest thing I've heard all day.

'The actress in *Vertigo* was beautiful,' Lisa says.

'You want to understand me?' I ask.

'Of course,' she replies. 'I want to know what's going on in your head. Your thoughts, passions and dislikes.'

'I haven't had anyone go to that kind of effort before. Besides Tony, and he is …'

I pause and then try and talk again but this time my voice is strained and it comes out in a coarse whisper.

'The character you mention in *Vertigo*, she wasn't really suffering from an illness,' I say, 'it was all fake, so that she and her lover could kill his wife.'

'What are you saying? That you and Tony plotted together to kill Ruth?'

I get up and walk over to the bars and place my hands through them. Lisa lets me take her hands in mine.

'I wouldn't want to be that heroine anyway,' I say. 'I'm more like Doris Day or Grace Kelly: the smart, blonde heroine. Or sometimes I'm more behind the scenes, like Hitchcock's wife, the loyal writer/editor Alma Reville.'

Lisa stares at me with her big, strange eyes. Her cold hands are still in mine.

'This wasn't how the story was going to end,' I say.

Fred comes up behind her and places a hand on her shoulder. 'Lisa, I want you to see a doctor. You've been through a lot today and you might be in shock.'

'I'm fine. Have they found him?'

'No, not yet,' he says. 'But we will.'

Lisa's face is puffy and red, but she holds herself well and her posture is admirable. A feeling of love for her swells through me and I realise I haven't felt this way about a friend in years. I don't want her to leave. I want her to stay here with me so we can continue to talk about films.

'I'll sort this out okay Patricia,' she says, but I

squeeze her hand tighter. 'I'm sorry. We all thought we were doing what was best, and now someone has died.'

I nod and let go of her hands as Fred leads her away. I hear him organise for a car to pick her up. He comes back to my cell.

'Well, I guess you're free to go,' he says as he unlocks the gate.

'How was Ruth murdered anyway? Strangulation?' I ask. He turns away.

'It's the way a few people have died in Hitchcock films,' I say. 'If I were to be set up, you know, framed, that would be the best way to do it.'

The policeman stares at me for a moment and then walks away. I sit back on the cell floor and put my head in my hands and start to cry. What would be worse, to be locked up in a jail cell, or locked up in a loony bin?

Tony is never found, and unfortunately the denouement doesn't end with me in my lover's arms, my hair in a neat golden bun, with pursed fuchsia lips, looking happily to the future. I've been in therapy for nearly a year and I haven't seen Lisa since that day at the Husky jail because she never returned my calls. In the first few months I used to cry about it, or tear out my hair, or lose sleep over it. I had finally found a true friend and then stuffed it up by getting her involved in a murder. I have thought about that night in the Husky bush every day since. I lost Tony, my lover, and Lisa, my friend. My shrink, Marsha, and I discuss the murder a lot. She's a classy redhead who is calm and caring. We work well together as patient and doctor. We also talk about escapism with films, and why I might use movies to avoid my problems. I've been put on a ban from watching or writing about films. Instead, I listen to music or bake to unwind.

Even so, I can't help feeling as though the murder, the arrest and everything that followed has happened because I'm in a murder mystery, and the fact that I wound up in therapy has put my movie on hold.

It's 10am and we sit in a small and cosy room at the Black Dog Institute in Randwick. It's like being in another world in here, comparable even to the Terry Gilliam film *Twelve Monkeys* or Foreman's *One Flew Over The Cuckoo's Nest*.

'There are still so many unanswered questions,' I say to Marsha.

'About the murder?' she asks me.

'Yes. For example, no one actually saw Tony or me kill Ruth. What if Tony blamed me because he actually believed I did it? And he called me the killer because he didn't do it.'

'You still see Tony as the good guy?' Marsha asks.

'It's a possibility. What if Tony had found Ruth's dead body and then rung Fred because he thought Lisa or I killed Ruth? And because Fred and Lisa were in on it together, they killed Tony? Tony was never found, dead or alive.'

'Why do you think Lisa would kill Ruth?' she asks. Marsha is writing down what I'm saying. A little line sits above her brow. I feel that she really cares about me, and perhaps it's okay to tell her things.

'That's what I can't figure out. The motive. But I have more unanswered questions.'

'What's spurred this on? Has something happened?'

'Yes,' I say, 'Mark came to visit me yesterday. It was the first time we've seen each other since before Huskisson. We discussed Lisa, and it made me question a few things. Firstly, why did Lisa get so involved with me? Mark said yesterday that he never told Lisa about Tony and Ruth. Mark and I had met Tony together at the Moon Tide film festival but he never realised we were having an affair. So, how did Lisa know about my affair then? Secondly, Mark also said that Lisa had approached him to be my assistant. Mark thought I was just a film buff, but he didn't think for a second I was mentally ill. Lisa made him so concerned that he went along with it. She has this persuasive way with people

155

you see, like Helen Bonham Carter in Sweeny Todd. Although she ended up dead. Helen that is. Not Lisa.'

Marsha looks up from her writing, frowning. I'm not supposed to mention films or actors or characters. I start to think about that night again. When Lisa came into the police station and spoke about the bush, that whole conversation could have been staged between her and Fred. Maybe Fred was in love with Lisa and prepared to do whatever she wanted. Surely, Lisa saying she saw Tony running after Ruth is not enough evidence to let me leave the jail cell when he did. Surely there is some kind of procedure that police have to follow.

'Pat, Pat,' Marsha says and I realise that I've been staring into space.

'You have to listen to me,' she continues. 'This is very important. You have to stop thinking about your life as a murder mystery. It's the only chance you have of a happy and healthy future. You're a smart, talented and beautiful girl and you could have a stable and steady relationship with a man who loves you, without all the drama of affairs and things.'

'But Marsha, drama is life. It's just got the dull bits left out.'

'Pat, you can only move on from Alfred Hitchcock, and Tony Walker, when you are prepared to give up the

156

drama.'

I nod and walk to the door. Our hour is up.

'Good luck,' she says as she gives me a warm smile.

'Thank you Marsha. I'll see you next week,' I say as I leave the cinematic world of *Twelve Monkeys* and *One Flew Over The Cuckoo's Nest* and enter into the real world.

RESPONSIBILITY

9

A HOUSE DIVIDED

BY J.R. McCRAE

The mood of the court shifted slightly as Dayne entered under escort. Servicemen whispered behind gloved ands. The General sat po-faced, looking straight ahead.

Dayne's uniform, showing signs of battle fatigue, had been pressed. His medal gleamed on his chest in all its untarnished glory. He passed under the lights to what served as a dock, the medal flashed. This did not escape the General's notice. He winced. Just days ago he had pinned it on Dayne's chest.

Court martial, summary court martial and execution for a hero who walked out on a battle, the General almost imperceptibly shook his head.

Dayne, a career soldier, had no qualms about killing. Soldiers did that. A good soldier gave his all! He had been mentioned in dispatches. How many times? The General tried to recall but lost count.

159

Bravery under fire, distinguished service; he knew how to rally his men to give their best. Dayne set the agenda, no risk too great, if his men's lives were at stake, if the advantage could be taken, ground won. A soldier's soldier. A born leader. What went wrong?

Dayne had done the unforgivable. In the heat of battle, he had turned and simply walked. A stray bullet glanced off his epaulet like he was charmed.

Under the shocked gaze of a speechless commander, Dayne passed through the ranks of his men and kept walking until the noise of fire dulled.

He walked into the command tent and surrendered his commission. Just like that.

****

Dayne always led; the angry, driven adventurer. Paul followed his older twin into whatever hell he led them. Paul followed, role undefined, his person malleable. He would just go where Dayne led.

Out on the lake in their uncle's skiff a storm hit. Both near drowned. Dayne, the ringleader, was lashed till he bled. It did nothing to deter him. Paul was forced to witness as his lesson. Dayne's eyes never blinked.

He took Paul hunting with their father's rifles. Dayne wanted bear. They found it, ranging in the woods at the back of the ranch. The bear turned and galloped at them. Dayne shoved Paul ahead around a tree, twisted and shot the bear through the heart as it reared to strike. Its dying blood-warm breath burst over them like the sigh of wind at winter's end. It fell and shuddered earth and rock.

Dayne took the great incisors. One for him, one for Paul, round their necks on leather he cured himself from its hide. The skin, head intact, carpeted their shared sleeping quarters.

There had been no punishment that time. The bear had taken cattle.

That winter the unthinkable happened.

"There's no help George," their mother's despairing voice drifted upstairs.

"I know Jessica, I know," said their father, resigned. "There 's no one else with your Pa gone. Damn your sister."

"George!" Their mother's voice ricocheted with shock off the stone walls of the ranch house.

"Damn, Jessica! We need you, and what does you sister do? Runs off with a no good soldier boy. Gets herself taken in the territories. He gets a medal she gets scalped and how's that help now?"

The boys could hear their mother softly crying. "She needs me…"

"She had the lot! Servants. Everything. And your no good Pa!" Their father cut short. The boys knew the streams of money trickled off East to Richmond, Virginia, to pay Pa's gambling debts, keep food on the table. Not enough for their grandmother's lifestyle, too much for her idle, flighty mind. Her demands became wilder, increased till their father refused another cent. A month gone, Pa was found with a bullet in his brain. The magistrate had contacted them. He had placed Grandmother in an asylum. Father had read the letter at the dinner table. Their mother, sobbing softly, her head hanging down on her bosom, made no comment.

"For her own good" he says. Their father sighed. "For her own damn good. Woman needed a hiding long gone!" Their mother's sobs loudened.

"STOP snivelling woman!" He put down the letter and thumped his fists onto the table so the crockery jumped. "What in tarnation do you expect ME to do?"

Their mother, as usual, said nothing. The usual silent warfare ensued over the following months, broken by bouts of swearing when their father lost patience.

Silence wore him down.

The first snows arrived, chill with their mother and Paul's departure. "It won't be long George." Her voice trembled. "Her health has never been good. You know

162

that. Paul will do well out there. They have fine colleges, a fine university. I need him, need someone, I.." Father's impatient kiss shut her up.

Mother hugged Dayne till he pushed her off, ranch hands watching, sniggering behind their hands. "I'm right, Mother! Paul will see to you, right, brother?"

The boys clapped each other on the back. The younger, gentler twin, Paul's eyes misted. Dayne didn't trust himself to speak.

He stood watching the distant train lights long after his father had mounted up the dray and left with the order, "Expect you in the hour. No later."

When even the imaginary echo of wheels on steel track had faded, he mounted and took his time back.

Without his mother and Paul's peace-keeping, Dayne grew angrier. He picked fights with the men, gave as good as he got and maintained a sullen silence round his father.

Letters arrived. They brought no comfort.

"She is putting on weight and so happy to see us! It is lovely. Folk are so refined. It's just like old times. The place is looking like a new pin! Mind, we only live on the bottom storey. We don't need more. Sissy Backer's housekeeper has a simple girl. The girl comes twice a week. You have to tell her EVERYTHING, but she works hard." There was no mention of home.

Paul's letter to Dayne told a different story. "We might as well be home. You know Grandmother treats Mother like Father always did. Demand, demand from sun up to sun down. God I'm glad I'm no woman. I'd like to take Mother away. The old lady's killing her. She sits and gets fat and gives orders and there's just mother and the Girl. Funny, no one gives her a name, just 'Girl'. Girl goes home at dusk and Mother has to cope till I get home from college. I swear Grandmother's like caring for a big baby. It's getting worse. She won't get around and her legs are seizing up. Doctor told her as much but she has this sick sly grin like she knows exactly what she's doing. Miss you, brother. Try and write."

Father sat by the fire holding Mother's letter, staring into the flames. Then he stood up, threw it in and stormed out. He spent the night in town. Next day, when he returned he smelled of strange perfume.

Letter after letter came with no mention of an end date. Father's visits to town increased.

The letters from Mother came less often, the stay more entrenched.

"Mother is so in need, so frail. George it is so sad. She needs me so much. I'm all she has poor pet. I think the Girl isn't simple, she understands well enough when she's looking at your lips even though she says naught but a cry if Grandmother strikes at her with the walking stick. She seems to be honest though. I have offered her to stay upstairs. I really need her here. Mother is getting heavy. We could do with Dayne's strong arms but you need him there."

Paul still wrote as regular but the longing for home dimmed. There was distraction. "I swear, brother, I never thought I'd call one of our own ugly. Grandmother's ugly. There I've said it. She has a meanness and a cunning and her temper is something to see. She has broken so much crockery we are now using the remnants of the best dinner service. I told Mother we should serve her on enamelware but she will have none of it. Only the best for her mama! Girl is my comfort. She stays here now and she is no simpleton. I've been teaching her. She can cipher and read now and her writing is fair. Don't speak of this to anyone."

Looking out the bay window in the direction of town, Dayne considered heading east. Then, with the thought of the woman dominated house, he shook his head. Women! Father's outbursts had subsided somewhat but the common talk had it he 'kept a woman' in town. As Dayne watched, a dust cloud moved along the road from town. Visitors were few. He fixed his gaze till he recognised his father's surrey and pair. He started to turn when a figure on the seat next to his father caught his attention. A woman, why was father bringing her here – a housekeeper? Too young, clothing too fine, father's fancy woman! He started back as the realisation hit. A whore! His father dared bring home his whore!

Dayne headed for his quarters and threw essentials in his duffle bag. Rumblings of war had been about. He had thought to enlist. The whore decided things. The new rifle with the sights, Father's toy, Dayne lifted it from its case in Father's study and was saddling up on his father's prize black stallion as the surrey pulled up to the front of the house. He headed down the back road, north, and didn't look back. As he cleared the property line, he heard a distant roar and smiled. Father missed the horse and rifle, not the son.

****

Soldiering suited Dayne neat as the fit of his uniform. Months passed in march time. Officer material was on short supply and he wrote the textbook. They kept on the move, town to town, bivouac in forest, in field, mud, slush and spring green. One more letter arrived from Paul, part torn, mud spattered. The postmark told of months travel.

"Well you sure did it this time brother, Father is

166

mad as hell. Can't blame you though. Word has it there is a housekeeper at the spread now, young, pretty. Mother is none too happy but she won't leave Grandmother. Pity.

I have my own concerns. Girl and I want to marry. No one will wed us here. Girl is what folks call mulatto. Before you react, think of Father's half-caste brother, Pelletier, by his father's wilderness wife, remember, the trapper from beyond the Great Lakes. He was good to us that one time he came. I've written to him. Girl and I want to head to Canada. They will marry us there. Mother is worn down by Grandmother. She may not last as long as her mother. But I cannot wait. They are conscripting all able bodied men here, even those in dotage and boys. If I don't leave now with Girl, my own family goes unprotected. You read aright. Girl is with child. We've hidden it best we can. Mother would throw Girl out on principle. Grandmother would have apoplexy. We must go now best we can and make Canada by autumn. Finding Pelletier may take time and time is running out. By the time you get this I hope to be gone. If you can, come, please come for Mother's sake."

Dayne wrote a few scant words of letter in return. He stuffed both in his coat pocket, threw his rifle over his shoulder and headed out to his men.

At day's wane, he rallied his men, one last time. A farm boy with red hair, one of his new recruits, fell gashed open in front of him. "Bastard!" Dayne fired at the soldier who turned, blood still dripping from his bayonet. The man looked up in Dayne's eyes as he fell. Recognition…

****

The house was quiet in the lull of afternoon. Grandmother snored noisily and Mother had collapsed into the sleep of soul weary exhaustion. Up the staircase Paul and Girl had everything prepared weeks before, awaiting such an opportunity. The donkey was tethered in the trees. Horses and livestock confiscated months before for the war effort.

Again and again their escape had been thwarted. Mother would force herself awake like a frightened young wife over her first born, watching the heave and fall of Grandmother's chest. She would sleep, finally. They would pull their things together fast, only to have Grandmother wake with yelled demands and throw the house to chaos.

Time had lapsed. The war crept perilously closer. Yesterday, the local guard had started door to door conscription of all the able bodied and many not so.

Today must be it.

Bags slung over shoulder, they reached the top of the great staircase. They were going down to the pantry to gather the last of their journey's supplies. Girl glanced out through the huge windows that looked down the gentle valley to town. The dust of horsemen caught her eye. Her fingers dug urgently into Paul's arm. He followed her gaze and pulled her swiftly back to the rear of the house. No taking the stairs now. Sheets tore off beds and strung together in a makeshift rope. He lowered Girl down first, with most supplies, whispering loud as he dared, "Head into the woods. I'll follow. If anything happens, keep going to Canada." She nodded as she bumped to the ground, scrambled up and headed to the trees. The slope was slippery with a rain shower. Girl slipped, twisted to protect a belly not yet noticeable to any but the most astute. A sharp cry! Her foot twisted under her. She looked helplessly up at Paul and tried to drag herself to the trees.

From the house two sounds mingled, Grandmother's yell for attention and a thunderous knocking at the door. Paul shimmied down the sheets, hurdled the makeshift rope out of sight and headed to Girl as the sound of horse hooves made him turn.

Next instant he was under guard and being hurried back to the front of the house and Girl was unceremoniously dragged back into the house, "Ma'am, you need to keep a better reign on your darkie here. She was headed to the woods and him after her." The laugh was dirty and Grandmother missed none of the implications. The barrage of language woke Mother, who stumbled in dishevelled and shrank back with embarrassment at the assembled group that greeted her.

Mother, to her credit, pleaded eloquently for Paul's release to them. "Pity, good sir! We have no man but my son to run this place. As you see, we are women and one an invalid. We…"

"You've darkie here! More than many with the wretches running north like hares before hounds. The Confederacy needs him more!" With that he turned on his heel and his men pulled Paul after them.

Paul's eyes met Girl's. "Trapper." And that was it.

****

The sky was turning. The long shadows reached down the mountain, invading the valley plain.

All day, Dayne had rallied his men in the thick of fire with a ferocity of those trained and consecrated to the arts of war. Sweat and blood ran in rivulets down the creases of his face. He licked at the corners of his

170

mouth, salt sweet and warm, a slightly meaty, sickly taste. His or that of the newly dead trod under his boots, blood's blood. He looked in the eyes of men he fought, unafraid to know his enemy. Others of his men flinched at this, young Jenkins, Bible Joe, Gramps Elshaw, conscripts, grit teeth soldiers fighting for their homes and families. These men shied from carrying the burden of that recognition, that moment when the man confronting you knows he has met his fate. They killed like desperate boys in the schoolyard, clenching eyes and flailing fists.

The day covered with blood, soaked the horizon long red. The ground stamped to mud. What grass there was, blood caked and rocks spattered. Any moment, the generals would sound retreat to night and bivouac, gather their dead and injured whilst there was still light to identify the uniform.

For Dayne, day's ended half finished, work lying in the cradle of the gun undone. Blood hunger, addictive restlessness, Dayne drove them stumbling tired into the very teeth of the enemy, calling and cursing them on. They were nearing the Confederacy eastern stronghold. Men fought their flagging and worn enemy with renewed vigour.

"We're damned," Bible Joe would mutter in his prayers before battle, "God help us."

171

****

The march into town took eternity with Mother's cries still ringing in his ears and Grandmother's curses. Stronger was Girl's look. At least, he knew, first opportunity she would go north. First chance, he would too.

Basic training amounted to the question, "Can you shoot?" The uniform was ill fitting and had a bullet wound in the coat as must have finished the previous occupant. He was herded north. First he knew of battle was the sound, bullets, canon, cries of the defiant and the dying.

He did what he had done all his life. Followed. He fired, ran, fired mechanically. Didn't dare look at the dead and dying in case he recognised what no man wants to see, his own fate staring back. The coat, spattered beyond recognition now, bore red badges of courage and mud caked thick.

Ahead was a pack of them charging down in a fury of blades and fire. The officer out front a blur of blue and blood. Then it was all around him.

One moment a red haired country boy was charging him, bayonet fixed, next he was twisting on the ground beside Paul, his guts spilling. Paul fired again. The body stilled. He swerved front to see the muzzle of the officer's gun discharge. The blue sky blackened over him, a blanket.

In the confusion at sunset, his body was gathered up with Union fallen and laid out with their dead.

"Sir!"

"At ease Sergeant." Lucas had the impatient edge of a man with other things on his mind. "What is it?"

"One of the dead men, sir. The boys thought it Dayne and brought it in. Uncanny alike. The bear tooth and the uniform so matted it could've been Union. But it ain't Dayne, sir?"

"Show me!"

They strode through lines of dead and wounded to a body whose barely recognizable coat in the half-light, bore two bullet holes, one old, one fresh with blood.

Lucas bent over and took the bear tooth on its thong of hide, clenching ii in his fist.

"Take it back man. Some mother needs to know her boy is gone."

He stood staring at the dead man till the Sergeant commandeered orderlies to carry the body over. Dayne had mentioned an incident ... A truth dawned, awful in its realisation.

****

173

"You know it's the firing squad," The General looked back at Dayne's commanding officer, Major Lucas, addressing him with more than a hint of concern in his voice.

The court had adjourned. Guilty.

"We found letters in his keeping. One from Confederate territory asking his help. One from Dayne himself, short but no mistaking: 'I'm coming, God willing. I'm coming.'

"The General's face and voice gave no ground.

Lucas tried again, matter-of-fact as he could, "It's thought the letter was from his twin out East."

"'A house divided against itself shall fall', Mark 3, verse 25." The General coughed. The anomaly of the medal and citations had not sat well with him. The man was an example. He must be an example now.

Lucas noted the set of the General's jaw. No mercy there. Dayne had followed Lucas up through the ranks. Try as he might to keep professional distance, this angry young man impressed him, no less because of his own troubled background.

The execution had been set for sun up. Lucas went to the enclosure that served as stockade. Dayne stood alone, hands tied. Lucas looked over his shoulder to the tether lines where Dayne's black stallion grazed a few scant feet away.

The shadows were long on the ground and dark was winging in on clouds. What were the chances? Lucas wandered over to the stallion and patted his neck. As dark swept in, Lucas relieved the sentry and slipped into the stockade.

Dayne registered surprise but said nothing. Lucas reached out and took the bear tooth round Dayne's neck in his hand, holding up the other as he did. In the last glimmer of light it was obvious. "Your twin. Why say nothing?" He pressed the tooth into Dayne's hand.

"I shot him. Just firing into enemy. There he was dying in front of me and me it was who pulled the trigger. My brother."

Lucas shook his head. "The letters. Girl, the babe - they have no one now. Do this for your brother." He glanced around. "The stallion's untethered. Go."

Dayne slipped through the dark shadows. A few strides and he was mounted and off heading north.

The General sat at his campfire musing at the dark. Something flickered at the edge of his vision A medal on a chest, the black stallion in full gallop.

"Marksman!" The General's arm swung unmistakably in the direction of the fleeing horse. The sentry fired. The rider shuddered and fell. The horse rode on.

Ashen faced, Lucas stared at the General. "Fetch the body, Lucas. You've saved us bullets."

Lucas strode the short distance to where he knew the body lay barely visible in the dark. He bent down. Blood trickled from Dayne's mouth but he was still alive. "Take these, Girl." His useless right hand held Dayne's bear tooth. His left hand struggled with the other around his own neck. He pocketed both and closed Dayne's dead eyes. After the war, if he survived, he'd deliver.

****

Girl was trying to help Grandmother onto the commode the day the officer came to the door. Paul had been gone scarcely more than a month.

Mother called out to Girl to answer the door. Grandmother yelled back , "Answer yourself you snivelling ninny! Girl is doing for ME!"

They could hear the rustle of Mother's gown as she headed to the door, heard the latch fall and the door swing back on hinges that could use oil.

Her faltering tones drifted to the back room where Girl, now having more difficulty hiding her condition, was struggling to seat the heavy old woman.

"HURRY UP! Stupid mute! HURRY UP! If I shit

myself you'll wear it!"

Girl stifled a sigh knowing Mother would be blushing with embarrassment as this last pronouncement echoed down the corridor.

Mother's voice floated down to them again. "Yes officer, what is the reason for this visit? As you see we are women alone, defenceless. My son…"

The officer, uncomfortable with his duty, interrupted, "Your son, Ma'am, is died in…"

His voice trailed off as Mother collapsed at his feet.

Down in the back room, Girl heard the thud and ran. She knelt by the ashen woman and looked up at the officer.

His muttered, "In the line of duty…" was drowned by abusive screams from the back room.

Tears trickling down her face she held Mother's hand. She was too still. The officer put his head on her chest then his cheek up to her nose and lips.

"Gone miss." The voice was kind for a southerner. He lifted Mother's prone form and placed her on the settee. "I'll fetch the doctor. You'll need certificate."

She nodded and looked over her shoulder to the backroom from where Grandmother's invective spewed down to them in a volatile stream.

The officer, stood, bowed and left in a hurry.

Girl struggled with Grandmother, ducking the old

woman's flailing efforts to hit her with the walking stick.

The rest of the day was a nightmare of waiting trying to deal with Grandmother's demands. She seemed to have no idea what had happened to her grandson nor a care for her daughter beyond demands to know why Mother was not carrying out her filial duty. The doctor's arrival did not make things easier.

He pronounced Mother dead. He told Grandmother he would send the undertaker. He knew the family plot, he said, and asked if arrangements had been made for Paul's body to be moved there.

"Well do it man! I'm a sick woman and all I have is this dumb idiot's care. What are you gawking at you ignorant darkie! Make tea for the doctor and me!"

"No, Ma'am, thank you. I'd best be off, making arrangements. " He nodded to Girl, "I'll let myself out!"

Alone with Grandmother, Girl rubbed her lower back as she tried to make dinner in between running backwards and forwards to attend to the old woman's incessant demands.

Alone that night, Girl let her emotions loose into the pillow. Paul's last word to her echoed around her mind as she drifted asleep. It was still night when she stirred. The candle still flickered hope in the dark room.

Her mind crowded with thoughts. She knew Paul wanted her to take their child and go to freedom, to not just survive, but live free, looking every man and woman in the eye with her head up. He would still want this.

She had kept what they packed tucked under her bed. Grandmother's snores drifted up, loud under the influence of her sleeping draught. Girl got out the bundles and added more things for the baby. She had taken to binding her stomach part to hide, part to protect in last weeks. She must go. War was on their doorstep. The Confederacy ingloriously losing.

How long would her journey take? She poured over an old map by candlelight, traced her fingers over the route north. She remembered the last known address for Pelletier. She wrote. During the undertaker's visit tomorrow, she would slip away, post the letter and go. There was still the donkey. She must go.

The old woman would argue over every arrangement, would drive the undertaker to distraction, would take time. Family pride and two bodies demanded this. Time, precious time Girl needed.

Girl checked everything twice before finally snuffing her candle and falling back asleep.

The morning came with driving rain. Grandmother swore and blamed, swung at her with the stick. The hours crawled passed. Girl almost didn't hear the undertaker's muffled knock. The thin man under the towering black umbrella looked as though he wanted to shelter all the bereaved under its black bat wings.

"Morning, Miss. Is Madame Ingenuie Dubonnet in?"

Girl looked at him blankly, then smiled and signalled him in. She had not heard Grandmother called by her name in years.

Grandmother's barked greeting, "You're late!" echoed up the stairs after Girl.

The rain drummed incessantly on the tiles. Her plans drowned in the widening puddles on the tiled landing at the top of the stone steps up from the lower carriage path. The steps were more decorative than anything. The carriage path made a circular drive right up to the entrance porch.

Girl descended with her things and sequestered them at the back of the house. The undertaker called, "Shall I let myself out, Ma'am?"

Girl hurried up but not before Grandmother let fly an invective that made the dour man blush. Girl took advantage of the man's discomfort and handed him her letter and a note, 'For the late woman's son, would you, sir, kindly post this?'

He nodded and left.

The undertaker would do what he did best, undertake – the coffins, the preacher, the funeral details, the hearse, even the flowers. It would be no sooner than the end of the week. Too long. The Union frontrunners could be upon them any time. Despite the Union abolitionist claims, many Unionists were as anti runaways as southerners. Confederate men on the run from the field were ragged, hungry and often enough, dangerous. She would work her way north where she could, while she could. It would be a long journey.

Overnight, the rain eased. But early morning the grey was lifting and the rain stopped. The ground was sodden.

Girl woke before sunrise and prepared. She crept downstairs and swallowed a hurried breakfast. Grandmother snored loudly. Girl made a last minute decision to take Mother's old winter coat. It was big enough that it would warm her when her belly swelled its fullest but it was much too small from Grandmother. She knew Mother would have given it to her with a caution 'Don't you let Grandmother know, you hear.' The way she had passed many things to Girl over the years. She took it off its hook and threw it on, for convenience.

Girl headed down, and was making her way to the where her things were stashed when grandmother sat up and saw her.

"How DARE you!" The abuse poured out.

Girl ignored her and with her bags slung over her shoulder headed for the front door. She was not sneaking out like a runaway. She was going a free woman. She opened the door. Something flew through the air and caught her on the side of her head. She fell, stunned. How long she lay there she didn't know but when her eyes flickered open Grandmother was standing over her, reaching down for her stick, which lay by Girl's side. Alarmed, Girl shuffled away, back, out the door, grabbing her things as she did. The old woman reached the stick and headed towards her. How had the woman fooled them this long? She could move, she was anything but helpless.

Girl staggered out across the tiles just missing a swipe of the stick. Girl made it to the stone steps and stepped down, down. Each step accompanied by the ominous tap of Grandmother's stick and every hateful, insulting, demeaning word in her considerable vocabulary. Girl got to the end of the steps and struck out on the carriage path. In the distance she could see a carriage coming from town, the undertaker's black carriage. Grandmother saw it too.

"THIEF! THIEF! RUNAWAY! GET THE DOGS!" Her screams carried out over the little valley.

Girl turned to head around back into the woods where the donkey was kept. The old woman, stood on the top step, shaking with fury. She hurled the stick. Two things happened, Girl ducked and the old woman fell. Girl ran.

****

Many months later, a man called Pelletier came in from the wilderness for supplies. "There's letters for you." The storekeeper droned. Pelletier looked up from the ledger where he was checking what he owed.

"Letters?" His half brother had never written, embarrassed by his father's indiscretion. No one else would. He picked up the letters and shoved them in his pocket intending to read them later. "I'll head to the tea rooms for a meal, Mac. Bundle it all together and I'll give you what I owe when I return."

Mac nodded.

Pelletier looked down as he headed out of the store, his left hand fingered the letters as if that would trace the mystery.

He did not see the young woman in the doorway holding a babe.

"Excuse, Madame," he muttered, the accent unmistakable. He looked up when she did not move.

She held her hand up to his face. Across the palm was tattooed a one word question,
'Pelletier?'

10

FOREIGN SOIL

BY JAN TURNER JONES

Zol put his hands over his ears and tried to drown out the sound of his parents arguing in Czechoslovakian. He could recite the litany by heart except for a new element – bankruptcy.

'…always showing off. You did this.' His mother's hysteria rose and rose. 'It's your fault, Wenzislas. This house has to go now and then we'll live in a unit like everyone else.'

'All sorts of people go bankrupt, Anna. It will pass.'

'You chose Brisbane, not me. It was a geographic lottery and now we have nothing but disgrace. I lost my life. I lost my country, my beautiful Prague, for this Stone Age society!' Her sobbing was loud and real. 'I hate this place . . . I hate it!'

'We came to save ourselves.'

'We should have stayed.'

'The communists would have killed me, Anna, or thrown me in jail.'

'Would that have been worse? There is nothing here . . . a dead place, no culture, no community.'

Wenzislas grabbed her shoulders and tried to quieten the screeching. 'This is our place, Anna. This is our home.'

'Home?!'

'Think of the boy. He's got to sit for his examinations next week. Think of the boy at least. This is the reality of our lives.'

She fell back onto the leather lounge and he looked at her and felt shame. My Anna, the most beautiful girl I ever saw, rich as well as beautiful. He remembered the early days when she was in love with his brashness and the risks he took to raise himself from a run-of-the-mill existence. Did you ever love me, Anna, just for myself, or did I provide the excitement that your smooth existence lacked? Your parents never accepted I was good enough. He watched her contorted face, still beautiful in spite of years of despair, and sighed deeply. 'It's my fault, Anna. That's the truth. I just wanted you to have the things you've always had, just wanted people to respect us.' She pushed his hand away and he stood up quietly and left the house as usual.

Zol came downstairs as soon as his father went through the door and sat on the edge of the couch as he'd done so many times. His father had given up on Matka's depression years ago and Zol knew his mother was his responsibility – providing comfort, making sure she was taking her medication, putting out clean clothes and underwear so she would at least look tidy, even combing her hair -- there was no one else. His mother grew quiet at last, brushing away tears and mucus with her hand. Seeing this once-elegant woman wiping her face like an urchin made his gut knot. He wiped her face with his handkerchief.

'Don't worry, Matka. I'll leave school and get a job. Everything will be all right.'

She shook her head violently. 'There are no tears left,' she said quietly, 'but if you walk away from school, I will kill myself. Your education is the only thing worth salvaging even though you now attend the state school. I ache, but your father and I will survive this. Our future is not important.'

'Don't talk like your life is over. You shouldn't do this all the time. This school's all right, better than Grammar in a lot of ways.'

'You belong to this place now, Zoltan. Go and do your study tonight. I want to stay here alone with my memories.'

'I'm not leaving you like this.'

'You always leave me like this in the end. Don't worry about me. I died a long time ago. I will only kill what's left if you stop going to your school – that's my contract. Tomorrow I will go to the clinic again and take the pills so my mind can keep my body alive until you are a man.'

Zol was torn. Once again the joint pressures of his father's financial problems and his mother's depression were a heavy weight on his 17 year old shoulders. 'You can be happy if you want to,' he told her earnestly. 'It's a good place and Dad's a kind man -- if you let him in.'

'It's a dead place and Wenzislas is weak.'

'He was important. You told me.'

'He was important once, but important people have a long way to fall. Now he's just a man of straw. Go to your study group and leave me alone with my memories.'

The room glowed with the last rays of a crimson sunset, but Zol knew his mother's darkness was immovable so, with a guilty sigh, he left her sitting alone in the fading light. He dragged the ornate front door open and looked at the sky and the river. People on hills all over Brisbane are probably calling out to one another to come and see how beautiful the sky is tonight. He stared at the colours for a long time before locking the door and leaving for the study group and safety.

Ernst Liddell stood next to the door and smiled. 'The others are here. Come in and we'll start.'

Zol sat through the maths tutorial without hearing a word and at the end of the session as the other students left the flat, he hung back.

'Is everything thing all right?' Ernst's words hung between them, an invitation for the boy to break. Neither man moved.

'You'll have to tell me,' Ernst said finally. 'I don't know what you want.'

'Can I stay here?'

'Why do you come for tutoring? I'm curious. You're strong in mathematics.'

'I've got to go somewhere.'

'Well come and talk to me, but I don't think you can stay. Have you had dinner?'

'I'm not hungry.'

'Everybody's got to eat. Come on.'

Suddenly Zol began to sob. For the first time in his life he stood defenceless in front of a stranger, unable to control the despair that was wracking his body. His distress continued and Ernst hesitated before going to the kitchen and walking back with a small glass. 'Scotch,' he said. 'Always works for me.' He handed the boy a tissue. 'Sit down.'

Zol wiped his face and took the glass, gulping the contents in one quick motion.

'That went down easily. Want to talk about it?'

He tried to tell his teacher how the fears and frustrations of his bleak existence were pressing in on him, tried to express his despair in words, but the words wouldn't come.

Ernst finally sat down beside him and put an arm around his shoulders. After a few seconds, he removed his arm and stood up. 'Believe me, Zol, this is one of the hardest things I've ever had to say, but I think you should leave now.'

'I don't want to go home.'

Ernst sat down again. 'You have to leave,' he said softly.

'Just for tonight.' He knew he was begging but he couldn't help himself. 'Please.'

'I'll get you something to eat.' The teacher went back to the kitchen but the smell of cooking made Zol nauseous and he vomited down the front of his shirt before he reached the bathroom.

Ernst stared at the mess. 'You had better take it off,' he said. 'I'll get you something clean.' He pulled the shirt over the boy's head and threw it in the bathroom basin and came back with a damp washer and

190

a white T-shirt. 'Here, clean yourself up,' he said frowning at the motionless boy in front of him. He sighed, 'Put the T-shirt on.'

Zol pulled the T-shirt on and walked back to the couch. 'Sorry,' he mumbled.

'It's all right. You don't do something like that on purpose. What's the problem?'

'Everything's a mess. Dad's going bankrupt and my mother's . . .'

'In hospital?'

'You know about her?'

'Your father mentioned it at the parent interview. She's still fragile?'

'Fragile . . . no, she's . . . mad and I'm responsible … No, I don't mean it.'

'It's all right, son. My mother was German. All these displaced Europeans full of angst and darkness, yes?'

Zol leant his head on Ernst's chest and the teacher waited until he calmed down. 'You have to go home now,' he said. 'You're a temptation I don't need around this place.' The teacher and stood up and took a backward step.

'I'll be okay. I'm used to it.'

Ernst took his student's hands in his own and held them tightly. 'You know Anthony, from the study group?'

Zol nodded.

'Do you like him?'

He nodded again, confused. 'He's okay.'

'He would be a good friend for you, very good I think . . . safe, approachable. Talk to him.' Ernst finally let go. 'Good luck to you.'

As Zol walked home, he looked up at the Southern Cross and felt safe. There you are, my St Christopher icon, first anchor on that confusing night when we arrived in Brisbane. He watched fruit bats wheeling across the sky and frowned. Why did I choose St Christopher? I'd finished travelling? Why am I even thinking about it now?

When he arrived home, Anna was asleep in her bedroom and his father was still out. Safe, for a short time. He went to the drinks' cabinet and studied the contents, choosing a bottle of malt whiskey and filling a glass. He sat on the leather lounge, site of so many parental storms, closed his eyes and let the fluid slip down his throat until the glass was empty. He enjoyed the burning sensation and the warmth spreading through his body and after the second glass, he went to his bedroom and fell across the bed and slept through the night for the first time in months.

The following day he searched for Anthony

Sheffield. He knew this was a foreign action for a loner like himself but he couldn't stop his restless need to find the boy Ernst Liddell had described as 'safe'. Anthony was seated against a wall away from the general cacophony, deep in conversation with a girl. He stopped and turned away, but the girl called to him.

'Want to be in A Midsummer Night's Dream, Zol?'

He shook his head in embarrassment and the girl stood up and left.

'Sorry to interrupt,' he said to Anthony.

'It's all right. Jess just roped me in to play Demetrius.'

'You don't mind?'

'Mind! I like it, acting and all that.'

'I'd die.' Just spit it out. 'I was wondering . . . do you want to come to my place to study maths?'

Anthony considered. 'Might be useful. Not my best subject. But why do you come to Liddell's? You always know the answers.'

'Bad idea maybe. Don't worry. My mother's crazy and my father's going broke. I shouldn't have asked.'

Anthony laughed. 'Sounds like a good place for a Stanislavsky student. Want to start today?'

'I haven't got a clue what you're talking about, but today's good.'

As soon as they walked through the door Zol moved to the drinks' cabinet. 'You want something?' He checked there no one was home and poured two glasses of whiskey.

Anthony was looking around with wide eyes. 'You own this?'

'Yes.'

'Wow!'

'It's just a house.'

'It's fantastic.'

He handed Anthony the whisky and the boy tore his eyes away from the richness around him and looked at the glass in his hand. 'You like this stuff?'

'Don't know, but it takes the edge off things. Sometimes I think if I stay in this house, my head will explode. It's like being trapped in a Czechoslovakian time-warp that's been transferred to Brisbane. I've never told anyone before, except Mr Liddell. Don't know why I'm telling you, but he said you were . . . '

'Go on. What did Liddell say about me?'

'That you were safe.'

Anthony laughed. 'Poor bugger. He's scared of his own shadow.' He looked around. 'You actually own all this?'

'My parents . . . but it's on the market.'

'Bet that tears you up.'

'I hate this place. I don't even feel like I belong in this family.'

Loud squawks filled the air and Anthony raised his eyebrows.

'It's Quetzalcoatl.'

'Now it's me who hasn't got a clue.'

'I'll show you. You might as well have the tour like everyone else. This room isn't Czechoslovakian OR Australian -- just over-the-top like everything here.' They walked through cut glass doors. 'Behold our conservatorium,' said Zol with his arms spread wide.

'Wow again!' Anthony looked around the light-filled room full of tropical plants and orchids and saw a macaw sitting on a perch at one end flashing its rainbow feathers. 'Why Quetz . . . whatever?'

'Because he's like everything else in this place – exotic. Quetzalcoatl was some sort of Aztec god.'

The bird flapped its wings for attention and its sharp cries filled the air.

'This is like a foreign film,' Anthony said turning in circles. 'I never knew anyone in Brisbane lived like this.'

'Yes, it's a house full of beautiful objects.' He picked up a wooden tube lying on the table and handed it to Anthony.

'A telescope?'

'Kaleidoscope. Hand-made by Belgian monks. Hold it up to the light and turn those wooden rings.'

Anthony held the shaft to his eye and gasped. 'Rainbow lights and crystals. What makes the patterns?' he asked eagerly turning the rings.

'Sheets of etched glass.'

There was a sudden crunch and Anthony pulled the object away from his eye with a horrified expression. 'I've broken it.'

'No you haven't. It's not broken. The wood swells and it sticks . . . because of the humidity. '

Anthony put the kaleidoscope down on the table with a relieved sigh.

'It's beautiful anyway. I just can't stop saying that word.'

'Everything here is beautiful and everything is flawed.'

Anthony frowned at him. 'No wonder those idiots at school don't understand you. You don't talk like anyone else.'

'Because I'm not like them. I'm still trapped in wog-land. From the time they dumped us at the Nissen hut at Wacol, nothing worked for my parents – not even this house. Some people never get away from their first place. They just hang on, too full of regrets to make the most of what they've got. I'm part of it too.'

'God, you sound so . . . old.'

'I was born old.'

'I'm not criticising. I like the way you talk.'

'I don't usually say much to other kids and they don't say much to me. It's easier than having to watch every word.'

'You're interesting.'

'You're different too, not prejudiced.'

Anthony laughed. 'Hope not. I try to keep an open mind so I'll be a better actor. I'm applying to NIDA. Hope they haven't got a prejudice against banana-benders!'

Zol looked at him confused.

'Acting school. What are you going to do next year?'

'Don't know. Engineering probably.'

The macaw screeched again and Anthony walked towards the bird with an outstretched hand.

'Be careful. He's a cranky bastard – don't think he ever got over being in quarantine for so long. Want to see the rest of the house?' Zol paraded him through rooms with silk drapes, paintings and expensive carpets.

'Is all this stuff real?'

'Most of it. The paintings aren't, but they've been done by real artists. Matka's a snob, thinks Brisbane people won't know the difference.'

Anthony chuckled. 'You ever brought anyone from school here?'

'Don't tell them about this. I hate big places, but my mother needs it.' He led Anthony through the rest of the house and out through French doors to the garden.

'Wow!' Anthony grinned. 'I know I'm getting boring, but I've never seen anything like this. I guess you have a gardener?'

'We used to have two. See how all those hedges down there are cut into geometric patterns? Dad brought someone out from Europe to set that up.' He looked at the far boundaries of the property. 'I always preferred the neighbours' yards. That one on the right is purple, all purple, when the jacarandas come out and the one on the other side's got a rain forest. That's what I'd plant. When we first came here, the kids used to climb up into those mango trees and play games and throw mangoes at me. You can still see their cubbyhouse in the middle. I wasn't allowed to go over there, but I sneaked out one night and climbed into the cubby -- even grabbed a mango to eat.'

'Did they cop you?'

'Only the fruit bats! Gave me a hell of a fright. Fell out and broke my wrist. Didn't tell anyone for two days, but it got so bad, I had to make up a story.'

'All this stuff -- and it was just loneliness.'

'It isn't so bad, loneliness. My favourite place is down there … the jetty … used to just sit in an old rowing boat and watch the water.'

'Catch anything?'

'Didn't try … just sat.'

'God, Zol, your parents must have big money.'

'Not really. Anyway, there's nothing left now.' He looked at Anthony. 'Seen enough? We'd better go up to my room – I couldn't stand another session with my parents right now. I always feel like Papa Bear.' He grabbed the whiskey bottle on the way through and led Anthony upstairs.

'So much space up here. My whole family could live comfortably in this room -- and you've got your own stereo and television!'

'Not much I like on TV, just a lot of noise, but it drowns out my mother on her bad days. Want to hear some Czech songs?'

Anthony nodded as he looked around. 'You've got a lot of stuff, Zol.'

'My father bought it to impress people.'

'In your bedroom!'

'I told you, there's always a tour of the house when businessmen come. My father tries to impress people the way he used to back home.'

'What does he do?'

'Imports things.'

'What did he do before?'

'He was in the government, something official and dangerous when the Commies took over. I can't remember anything, but my father said that Matka, my mother, used to play the piano and sing. I remember her songs –- they're like these.' They listened to the record for a time and Zol sighed. 'So here we are. Want to do some maths?'

'You screwing anyone?'

Zol looked at Anthony in surprise and shook his head. 'Are you?'

'I've done it with Jess.'

The feelings Zol had tried to suppress for the last few years were bubbling dangerously close to the surface. 'What's your family like?' he asked to divert the energy. 'As messed up as mine?'

'Normal. I'm the only one who doesn't fit, but they seem to like me even though I go to dancing and drama. I just get a hard time from the kids at school sometimes.' He smiled and shrugged.

'Want to start on the maths?'

Anthony shook his head and moved towards him and entered his space and the two of them stood

200

together breathing. Finally he reached out and undid the knot in Zol's school tie, followed by his own, and pulled both ties from around their necks and dropped them on the floor.

'I didn't ask you to come for this. That wasn't the reason.'

'There doesn't have to be a reason.' Anthony undid the buttons on his shirt and Zol finally shook off his inertia and worked clumsily on his own shirt.

'You want this?'

He nodded and they flung off their shirts and fumbled with belt buckles. They fell on the bed and experimented in dizzy cycles until the heat in Zol's head cooled and he felt such a sense of peace that the feeling was outside his experience. They lay still at last and Anthony stroked his lover's back. 'You're a good looking guy, just like me!' He laughed at himself. 'We'll both have to get out of Brisbane one of these days. Jess is fun, but this is better.'

'How did you know, I mean . . . about me? Is it obvious?'

Anthony shook his head. 'Liddell picked us though. Sent us to do what he's scared of doing.'

'I suppose so. I'll never be able to look him in the eye again. Do you want to do some maths now?'

Anthony threw back his head and laughed and they

wrapped their arms around each other's body. 'Jess should have cast me as Oberon. I like this.'

'You want to go for a swim?'

'Swim!'

'There's a heated pool and sauna in the basement.'

'Yes, yes, yes. We can do it in the sauna!' Anthony grabbed the whiskey bottle and slid across Zol's prone body and they both took a swig. 'All gone,' he said regretfully.

There was a sudden gasp and they turned in unison. Wenzislas stood in the doorway watching them, his eyes flowing over the naked bodies, the empty bottle and their clothes flung across the floor.

'Your mother has gone to the clinic, Zoltan,' he said softly, closing the door.

'Oh God, what'll we do?' Anthony said panicked.

'Don't know. This is all new.'

'Want me to stay?'

'He's not violent or anything. Pretty apathetic. Sad.'

'Sorry if it's going to cause trouble.'

'It's about the only thing in my life I'm not sorry about.'

Anthony dressed quickly, and they hugged. After he left, Zol stood up slowly and pulled on a pair of shorts. He went to his father's room and knocked on the door.　　　'I have to speak to you about this, Dad, about everything that's happening. Can I come in?'

Wenzislas was silent for so long that Zol put out his hand to open the door. He paused, realising he had insufficient courage to turn the handle uninvited. Grateful for his father's silence, he turned to walk away.

'Do your study, Zoltan, and go to bed. Nothing that has happened since your mother and I came to Brisbane is your fault. Nothing.'

He walked back to his room unsure whether he was pleased or upset by his father's quiet reaction. He felt he should go back and act responsibly and speak to his father. He returned to his room instead and picked up his clothes and attempted to straighten the rumpled bedding. He stopped midway to drag a sheet off the bed and hold it against his skin, pressing his nose into the soft material. I can still smell him. He stood clutching the sheet, trying to recall the rush of freedom he had just experienced and as he picked up the empty whiskey bottle he wished there was a shot left.

When he walked through the school gate the next morning, fearful that Anthony would be too embarrassed to face to him, he saw the youth waiting.

'What did your father do?'

'Nothing. I don't think he'll mention it again.'

Anthony looked relieved. 'I guess we'll just have to find somewhere else to study,' he said smiling.

After school Zol went straight home and found his father's bedroom door shut. Don't you crack up too. I'm used to Matka, but I won't cope if you both fall into the big black. He went to the kitchen to make Wenzislas a sandwich and watched two little girls next door laughing and calling to each other as they climbed around the big mango tree.

Upstairs again, he knocked before pushing his father's door open. The upturned chair attracted his gaze immediately and he stood unmoving, carefully balancing the tray, mesmerised by the expensive leather shoes dangling in front of his eyes.

Zol understood straight away that Matka was lost too. He knew irrevocably that nothing he did from that point on would make the slightest difference to the final outcome. He stood watching his father's shoes, willing himself to cry, or at least drop the tray, but the only feeling he could identify was one of relief, relief that all the years of pain, guilt and responsibility for his parents were over.

He lowered his gaze finally and stared out through the window at the river and the trees. He liked living in Brisbane, always had. He remembered the first hot week when they'd left the Nissen hut behind forever and climbed into a Black and White taxi for the journey to New Farm. He smiled as memories of the sagging river flat, complete with flies and ants, spiders and cockroaches, filled his head. Brisbane was his place. He could relax at last and just be like everyone else.

DEATH

11

GROWTH

BY S.M. JOHNSTON

June 28, 2010

Eleven hours in a car. Stiff and tired, I look over at my husband. I can't do this alone. I haven't seen my parents since January – six months. The car is snug and warm, but the outside temperature gauge on the car display panel reads much colder. Not that the winters in Queensland are freezing.

My husband hands me his new phone. It has inbuilt GPS. The novelty is a nice distraction. I watch the purple line and blue arrow guide us towards my parents' house. It's not long now as the map guides us past the hospital. After turning right, a small flag signalling our destination appears on the screen. Traversing the winding road, we arrive and the car swings into the driveway.

Butterflies flitter around my stomach. Will he look any different? He looked fine six months ago. He sounds fine whenever we talk on the phone. The reality is he probably wasn't fine six months ago. But we'll never know.

The gravel at the top car-space groans in protest as our SUV sneaks in. I want to rush down the driveway, throw my arms around Dad and burst into tears. But I know that's not what's wanted, or needed. I have to be strong.

I hover around the car, waiting for my husband to get what he needs. When I can wait no longer – he's always so slow – I bundle our sleeping son out of the seat and over my shoulders before tentatively making my way down the steep driveway. I tread carefully hoping not to slip in my thongs.

My mother waits at the door, eager and on edge. "Sorry we couldn't come up to meet you. It's just gotten too cold."

I nod, feeling the weight of my five-year-old bearing down on my shoulder. "It's okay. I understand."

Inside I catch my first glimpse of Dad. He looks the same at a glance, but I'm hardly in a position to judge with the bulk of a young child obscuring my

208

view. I negotiate my way through the lounge room, dining room and kitchen to the spare room where the boys will be sleeping and lay Jack down in the centre of the queen-size mattress that's on the floor.

"Tanya, don't put him in the middle," my mother frets. "Otherwise Big Bro won't fit."

I look at Mum curiously. "Lucas isn't with us. He comes down on the plane tomorrow." Had I forgotten to tell Mum our eldest son wouldn't be with us? No, she just has other things on her mind.

With Jack safely snuggled under the blankets, I go back out to the kitchen to say my hellos. Dad moves in for a hug. Instinctively I want to cradle him as though he's made of china, but I flinch slightly when I brush against his stomach. I don't remember his beer-belly protruding that far out.

I step back to survey him. The differences are subtle; someone who sees him every day wouldn't notice the change. His beard no longer shows any signs of his former redhead status; arms and legs have diminished in size in direct proportion to his increased girth. Around his neck there are increased lines. But it's his colour that stands out. There's barely a difference between his white beard and his skin. His freckly complexion has disappeared completely.

Sitting down opposite him at the table, I remain

mesmerised by his lines and paleness.

"You should have seen him two weeks ago. He looked like Casper the Ghost," Mum remarks as though she has read my thoughts.

I don't let my horror show. This is better?! He looks like a ghost now.

"He looks much better since they put those three bags of blood in him," she continues, oblivious to my shock.

A yawn escapes. "Do you guys have any cocoa?"

"Yes." Dad springs up. "What do you want?"

"A hot chocolate please. Nick, do you want one?" My husband sits beside me in "zombie mode"; a side effect of driving for eleven hours. He manages to shake his head.

The conversation slips away from me, my responses on autopilot as I watch Dad flit around the kitchen. He grabs a Jump-Rope-For-Heart mug that we had gotten years ago when we fundraised for the program - when I was young, when we were together, when we were a happy, healthy family.

"How do you have it?"

"One coco, one sugar," I reply.

Dad pulls two jars from the cupboard, one brown, one white. He put a teaspoon from the white jar in, then pauses, and tips it back in before returning the jar to the cupboard and pulling a new white jar out.

Was the sugar off? I think to myself. They don't use much sugar with Dad's diabetes. Then I realise he almost gave me his artificial sweetener by mistake.

He adds a teaspoon from each of the jars, and then pours in a small amount of boiled water before stirring vigorously. I'm a bit perplexed when he then adds copious amounts of milk and heads to the microwave. Not how I make cocoa, but then again we don't own a microwave.

"How hot do you like it?"

"Warm."

Dad brings the mug over to me, placing it on a coaster. I touch the cup – it' so hot – and then dip my pinkie into the coco – it's warm. "Perfect Dad."

A tired Nick excuses himself and heads to bed. That triggers the discussion.

"Do you know my specialist appointment is on the…" Dad trails off as he goes to check the calendar.

"The eighth," I finish for him.

Mum shifts uncomfortably in her seat. Normally it's just her and I talking about this kind of stuff.

"I must have had the cleanest ears ever. You know they check your temperature and blood pressure every minute for the first five minutes, then every half an hour over the five hours. And they check your temperature in your ears." Dad grins like a Cheshire cat, which baffles me.

"When you are getting ready for the examination you have to lie on your side." It must help him to talk this through.

"And you bite on a ring, which is where they feed the camera down. I already had the shunt in," I shudder as an image of Jack as a baby flashes in my mind, "from the blood so they put the anaesthetic in there. I kept thinking hurry up and knock me out, hurry up and knock me out.

"Then I felt it going cold up my arm and thought again hurry up and knock me out, hurry up and – oh the ring's gone, it must be over. It was that quick." He still looks so pale to me.

Mum totters away from the table and returns with her knitting. It's a blanket that began its life from Grandma's left over tapestry wool. She died on June 3, only two weeks before my parents got the bad news – to lose your mum, then this.

Yawning again, I excuse myself and go to bed so I can get up early for the gym the next day.

June 29, 2010

My watch's alarm is muffled under the bedspread.

I'm cold and tired, but I know I have to get up. I rifle through my bag for something to wear to the gym. Too cold for shorts, hmmm fat pants; trackie-dacks it is. I slip into the velour track pants and put on the polo shirt Mum gave me. After slipping on my socks and joggers, I wander out into the lounge room.

"Morning," I say as cheerfully as I can muster before continuing to the spare room. I scoop Jack up and cuddle him to me as I make my way back through the kitchen, dining room and lounge room areas to get to where my husband's still sleeping. Carefully I lay my precious bundle down, but his little eyes pop open and a cheeky grin appears. I guess he's coming with me to the gym.

"Do you want to stay here with Daddy or come with me to the gym?" I already know the answer.

"With you."

The four of us head to the car. Dad has been M.I.A. from the gym for the past few weeks. We don't speak on the way there. My mind keeps wandering.

It's only a short drive to the gym. I steer Jack to the children's area and let him pick out a show to watch. The Magic School Bus soon rings out at the front of the gym. I make a beeline for the cross-trainers – my exercise options are limited due to a healing stress fracture in my left leg. But at least from here I can see

213

straight down the hall to the children's area.

I place my water-bottle in the holder and begin the mid-air jogging motion, intently trying to keep to myself. Thankfully there aren't many people here. But still, my eyes work hard to avoid people's faces.

Jack's blonde hair bobs around as he explores the fort. As I continue to watch my son have fun, I notice my father moving away from the gym area and towards the sofa just up from the play area is. Is he okay? My mind races and I resist the urge to sprint over to him. I know it will embarrass him if I cause a scene. Mum joins me in the cardio area and signals she's just about done.

My thirty minutes are up, so I grab my things and head towards Dad just as Jack is trying to let himself out through the magnified gate.

"I'm done. Mum only has a few minutes left." I release the latch and set Jack free. Mum joins us so we head to the car.

On the way home we go past the hospital again. I look at the bleak grey building. They're expanding and the front is cornered off for construction. Then I see it, the sign – "Did you know that 34% of blood is used to treat cancer". When I get home, I promise myself.

I cannot believe how much our lives have fallen apart since Jack's birthday.

June 18, 2010

"Happy Birthday to you, happy birthday to you, happy birthday dear Jack, happy birthday to you," My husband, eldest son Lucas and I all chorused.

"Hip-Hip, Hooray, Hip-Hip, Hooray, Hip-Hip, Hooray."

Jack looked at us with a loopy grin then tore into his first present, wrapping paper thrown mercilessly all over the bed.

"Oh! Lego!" He pushed the box an inch from my face. Gently, I moved his arm back and smile.

"Open your next one, it's from me," Lucas said, puffing out his chest.

The sound of ripping paper filled the room as the three of us eagerly watched for Jack's reaction. Of course the figurine Lucas picked out was exactly what Jack wanted and the tearing of wrapping paper was replaced with the packaging being ripped to shreds.

As the boys bundled off the bed, I collected up the rubbish and headed out to the kitchen to start breakfast. Toast with vegemite was Jack's favourite. I trimmed the crusts off and put the plate on the table, then moved onto lunches.

Jack was first out, minus clothes. Dancing around

215

to a cartoon theme song, he ignored his toast and school uniforms waiting to be worn. I walked into the lounge room and grabbed the remote, clicking the off button. The dancing stopped, but the breakfast remained untouched.

"Ah, you made me some toast. Thanks, Mum," said Lucas, sneaking a look at Jack.

"No, it's mine!" squealed Jack, finally getting his still bare backside onto his seat. He nibbled at the edges to prove it.

Lucas walked towards me in his uniform, then stood toe-to-toe with me, grinning. He was enjoying his recent rapid growth spurt that left him a few centimetres taller then me.

"Yes, yes, you're taller than me now," I poked him gently. "Now you'd better fix yourself some breakfast."

"Can I have eggs?"

"No."

"Why not? It's Jack's birthday, it should be a special breakfast."

I raised an eyebrow. "We've run out. You'd better get moving. I don't have time to give you a lift this morning. You too Jack, better keep eating."

With the lunches finished, I made a start to the bedroom to get changed. Strong arms wrapped around me as I rounded the hallway.

"Hey beautiful." Nick's blue eyes bore into mine, but his hands moved south.

"Nick, cut it out," I giggled. "The kids could come around the corner."

"I don't care." He never broke eye contact.

I batted his hands away with a grin. "No time for your shenanigans this morning." Sauntering off down the hallway, I called out, "But maybe later tonight."

Quickly I got in my work clothes, a black pin-stripped skirt, pink satin-feel blouse and a tailored jacket. After slipping on my heels, I straightened my skirt and returned to the kitchen.

"All right, I'm off--"

"Yeah," interrupted Lucas, "We can smell you from here."

Ignoring his comment I continued, "Have a good day, especially you birthday boy." With that I planted a kiss atop Jack's head, then Nick's cheek (Lucas has decided he's too old for his mother's kisses) and walked out the door.

No phone call this morning from Mum and Dad – That's odd, I realised as I marched down the backstairs and made a mental note to give them a call from work.

~*~

"Hi Mum, it's me."

"Oh, hi honey." Mum sounded a bit flustered,

which was normal for her.

"So, we will be home at about six tonight if you wanted to call for Jack's Birthday."

"Sure thing."

She had to go and I felt hollow.

~*~

"I'm so sorry. I completely forgot," Mum began to explain after Jack returned the phone to me. I tried to take it in as Mum then told me that Dad was going in for a blood transfusion. His iron count was low. He had some health problems with blood pressure and diabetes, but I wasn't sure why he'd need a blood transfusion.

After saying our goodbyes I headed out to the lounge room and opened my laptop. Jumping onto Facebook, I relayed parts of the conversation to my friend, Mickey, in a message before beginning my regular sloth night.

I just wanted to drop you a line of thanks - where people couldn't all read it. You know my gran died, well my dad is now in hospital requiring blood transfusions. His iron count is really low. They are doing tests on Tuesday. I am worried for Mum as well. This is the first time apart since they retired.

On top of that, lots of other little and some big things have been going on like my car window got smashed and some other family issues that I don't really

want to go into but the support I have gotten from you has really helped keep my sanity this month.
Cheers
Tanya

Mickey had been my rock. Somehow, just writing the words made me feel better. I was sure it would all work out.

June 19, 2010

My shoulders ached from being hunched over a keyboard at work. And yet I found such release online at home. With the boys fed, bathed and in bed, and Nick preoccupied with a computer game, I indulged myself and went online.

My email messages were always the first thing I checked. There was a message notification. I opened my Facebook messages and saw Mickey had replied:

Oh Tanya ... When it rains, right? Wow ...

I totally get the stress of medical stuff ... goodness, it's so awful ... your poor dad and poor family! Any time blood transfusions are required, that's serious stuff. That scares me. And you haven't even had time to recover from your gran.

It's amazing too, I've discovered, that sometimes we are

okay with dealing with the big issues ... but it's those little every day annoyances and buggy things that push you over the edge--ya know? That make you feel like you're about to lose your sanity? Ugh ...

Dang, Tanya ... I'm so sorry you're dealing with such hardship. Just even thinking about it makes me sick. To think of my own dad in that position about does me in ... and your poor mum--and you! Having to carry the worry and stress that doesn't go away. I hope they'll find answers soon and that he'll be fine.

Even though it's nasty tough right now, I already can feel your strength and know that you'll use this hardship for good. Sorry if I sound cheesy, but I mean it.

Man, I'm sending the love and sympathy, and as much empathy as I can. Hopefully this craziness will all be a blur ... love to your poor family. You guys deserve a break! I'm totally here if you need an ear.

I reread the message. It can't be that serious! I pushed the thought down.

June 20 2010

I tried to process what Mum just said. They found a tumour in Dad's stomach.

"Dad didn't want you to know. But he told Mary

this morning. Are you going to be okay to tell Nick?"

The words started to sink in. Dad was sick, my sister knew, my dad was sick.

The tears won and welled over my eyelashes. I stumbled out of the room and handed the phone to my husband and suppressed a sob. Nick looked at me, confused, before putting the phone to his ear.

I curled into a ball on the back steps sobbing. No, no, no, no no! I was brought back to reality by a small hand touching my shoulder.

"Did Daddy make you sad?" my now five-year-old asked as only a babe can.

"No sweetie. Mummy's daddy is sick."

With the surging emotions calmed I returned to Nick. He was simply listening as Mum filled him in, occasionally acknowledging with a "yep." I needed to know what was happening and motioned to Nick that I wanted the phone back. He handed it to me after saying his goodbyes. It felt cold in my hands.

Mum told me there would be tests tomorrow. We had both forgotten what else was important about tomorrow.

June 21 2010

All I can think about was Dad going into hospital.

I muddled through some emails, trying to get my mind focused on work. It could go one of two ways. If it started in his lymph nodes then it'd be six months of chemo and possible recovery. If it started in his stomach then it was just time. How crazy was it when you were rooting for chemo?

I couldn't stand it any longer and called Mum.

"Hi, Sweetie." She didn't wait for me to respond. "I can't talk now, Dad's about to go into surgery.

"Okay, sure thing, Mum. Talk to you later." The disappointment was hidden from my voice.

For a moment I sat unmoving, shell-shocked by the whole situation. Finally, I flipped through my diary to try and get my mind on something else. I looked at today's date and saw it was Mum's birthday. How could I forget? I wrote a note on my hand so I wouldn't forget to call her tonight. Regardless, her birthday would be forever tainted from now on. It would always be the day that sealed Dad's fate one way or the other.

June 23 2010

Again, I fidgeted for most of the day. Dad's appointment was at 9:30am for the results of his biopsy. By lunchtime I was a mess. My emails were making no sense as I read them. Maybe I'd have been better off not being there. I went to leave as many times as I contemplated calling my parents to find out what was happening.

Finally I got a text from Mum – Dad is asleep, call after 4pm. I texted back immediately, hoping to glean some information. Are you okay? Her response was non-committal. I was about to go into a teleconference so I couldn't call.

For the next two hours I rubbed my tongue on the roof of my mouth to push back the tears – a trick I learnt from Australian Idol. It wasn't foolproof as occasionally tears formed.

The Regional Director, Bruce, was in the room with me on the teleconference. It didn't help that he looked so much like Dad, another 'ranga with a feisty temperament and a no-nonsense approach to life. I was worried he would notice the redness in my eyes and how little I was contributing. The last thing I needed was concern from someone because I was ready to fall in a heap.

I checked the time. 3pm. I excused myself from the teleconference, ducked back into my office and closed the door. The rugby league team I coached had their grand final game at 4pm. I was not going to be able to concentrate if I didn't know. I dialled Mum's mobile, hoping that wouldn't wake Dad.

"Hi Mum."

"Hi Lovie." Her voice gave nothing away and my hope soared.

"I hope it's okay to call now. I have football at four," I explained.

"That's okay."

"So, what's the news?"

"It's not good. It's cancer – the worst kind." The words took the wind out of me. I started to lose track of what she was saying. I just knew it was the worst case scenario.

Robot-like, I thanked Mum for telling me then packed my things and headed to the car, making sure I had my sun glasses. They were on before I even got out the door. My vision started to blur and I cried harder than I ever had in my life.

My tears continued all the way to the rugby league grounds.

~*~

I watched my son, Lucas, head down to rugby union training – Wednesdays were busy for him with a league game then union training – the tears welled again. My team listened to me, played hard and pulled through. We won the grand final. I even managed to keep the tears at bay.

But as soon as I was alone, I let the shields down

and started lamenting the losses to come. Not his death, but the events he would miss – not walking my sister down the aisle, missing my sons become men. He'd never know what careers they would have, who they would marry or see great-grandchildren. Two weeks ago I lost my last grandparent and now I knew I was going to lose a parent. I cried all the way home.

August 2 2010

I try to look anywhere but at the needle and not to think about the events that have happened since Jack's birthday.

"So, what made you decide to want to give blood?" The nurse is peppy, not knowing that is the second time I've been asked that today.

"I don't want to talk about it." She looks at me apologetically, but taken aback. I rubbed my tongue against the roof of my mouth and wish the tears away. But I fail, miserably.

She searches my arms without success.

"Lyn, I can't find the vein. Can you look at this?"

A new nurse appears. "Sure." She looks at my chart and smiles. "So, what made you want to donate blood?"

I shake my head tearfully. They look at each other

confused. Lyn taps inside my arm, hoping to raise a vein.

"I'm just going to get some heat pads."

She doesn't take long to return with warm heat pads and places them on my arms. After a minute she peaks, but she still can't see a vein.

"Shirley." A nurse in her forties pokes her head out of a room. "Can you give us a hand?" Lyn then turns to me and continues soothingly. "Shirley has done this for years. You'll be right." She pats my hand reassuringly.

The other nurse, Shirley joins us. Her eyes narrow at my distressed state. All I can think of is Dad.

"Right," Shirley says after inspecting my left arm. "You will feel a pinch."

It's more than a pinch and I grimace. Tears flow, but not from the pain.

"Are you alright?" asks Lyn.

I muster a nod.

Lyn and Shirley look at each other sceptically and then they leave me be to fill my bag of blood.

12

I WILL SAVE YOU

BY BEAU HILLIER

Dom does not go immediately to Jean's grave once he passes into the memorial garden. He only barely remembers where it is. He instead takes a circuit around the grounds, seeing the way religion separates people, the Catholics over here and the Methodists other there; and the way money defines memory, with some thrown into a mausoleum and others given a memorial, a spot near the trees, or gathered around a lily pond. There's a morbid curiosity; which ones had the rich families, and which ones could only barely afford the burial service? And the ponds, white and sparkling in the sunlight; Dom wants to know how many urns have been emptied there, and whether the ashes of people from opposite walks of life mingle under the water, moving with the sediment, dancing with the tiny currents caused by wind and goldfish. Are the goldfish even meant to be

227

there?

Neil has been doing the same thing; they run into each other in the middle of a pattern of hedges that feels more like a maze. 'I was beginning to think you wouldn't be here,' says Neil.

'Same here,' says Dom.

'Shall we?'

'I don't know if I can.'

'And that's why I'm here.' Neil's self-consciousness shows. He moves as if the dead watch and appraise him, and tries to shrug it off with a smile and a gesture to keep walking, not in the right direction but, with Dom's reluctant navigation, edging relatively closer.

'So what do you have planned for the radio show tonight?' asks Dom. His voice echoes in his own head.

'You can come in again if you want and find out.'

'That might be an idea.'

Neil stands taller, and brushes his prosthetic hand over larger tombstones standing rigid and silent; he looks at each one of them, his eyes wild and forceful. Dom cannot meet his gaze, as Neil is too occupied with reading every tombstone he comes across, reciting the names – 'James Paramore … Richard Prescott …' – and touching them, blessing them, and maybe in a world beyond Dom's senses they follow him, and an assembly gathers to hear Neil Loewenberg speak to them with a voice like a siren's song.

'Do you know anyone here?' Dom asks softly.

'No. But I feel like I should.'

Dom's hands are clammy. They're close. After however many months, and it strikes Dom that he may have brought Ian with him. He might catch on to something, although a toddler wouldn't quite bow in reverence. A son has the right to visit his mother, even if only by a slab of stone and the fright of realising she lies six feet under the ground, trapped in a box.

'She's over there.'

'Lead the way.'

Dom would have preferred it if Neil led the way. It would not have surprised him if Neil went straight to it, drawn by intuition. But Dom leads, and he moves along the lines, edging tenderly through as if moving through a narrow corridor, and there is Jean Milford; a modest plaque on a slab of stone, with a name and two dates and the epitaph.

'I can move away for a little, while you say hi.'

'I won't be saying it out loud.'

'I think you should.' And he moves down the line, his prosthetic hand dangling, waving over the slabs of stone, whispering the names. It seems so systematic, cataloguing the names and listing them in a mental rolodex.

Dom turns back. The plaque stares back at him, and he wants a picture of some sort under those empty words, something that could say a thousand more words, about what a mother she was and how she always moved with an angel's grace, a throwback to dancing days.

Neil's movement, in a short distance before him, makes him look up. He is still in his trance, moving down the lines, appraising a rank of memorials and somehow, incomprehensively, finding a way to love every one of them. The eyes siphon all the details, and Dom doesn't doubt that Neil could remember every one of them, a photographic memory that etches emotions into granite and erects vast walls of experience, summing up the will and versatility of humanity into a single mind.

'Sorry I haven't visited.'

Jean waits, wanting him to say more.

'I know you want me to say I love you, and I do, I love you, but that's not really what I came to say. I don't really know why I had to have someone else drag me along here. I shouldn't really be so scared.' It takes so long to speak, such an agonising amount of time to get everything, even the simple stuff, out into strained and mangled sentences. Surely Jean is frustrated by now; he woke her for this?

'I am scared. The way sixteen years of my life vanished like that. Ian is here, but I barely register him sometimes. Mya's off in Sydney doing her own thing; funny, you were more of a mother to her than her actual mother.'

Neil completes his small circuit, and comes back. They meet eyes. Neil nods, and kneels at the side of the grave, his real hand touching the plaque and tracing the epitaph as he speaks:

'Jean Hannah Milford. You were 41, neither too young to miss life nor too old to let regrets pile up. I like to think you left with dignity and beauty, whatever happened in the last moments.'

'You're being dramatic,' says Dom, in a smoker's strained voice.

Neil makes no sign of hearing him. 'I believe in God, so I believe He has taken you in His embrace. You are not dead. You live on beyond us and with us.' He stands up, and shivers under the scorching sun. 'No one here is dead. The only dead ones are those who refuse to live properly.'

'What the hell are you talking about?'

Neil whips around, grabs both of Dom's shoulders; the flesh hand digs in deeper than the hard false hand. Neil's never explained what happened to give him a false hand. 'That's why I wanted you here, Dom. I want you to look at the resting place of Jean Hannah Milford and promise her you're going to live again. Tell her that you'll let God spare you from eternal death.'

'What the hell do you mean? Death is eternal.'

'No, wrong. Death is a change but not an absolute destruction, and eternal death happens in the mind, happens in apathy and loneliness and the individual –'

'Speak slower, I can't keep up with you.'

'Tell her,' he says, teeth flashing like fangs. The eyes bore into him; everything he just sucked up across the cemetery, all the names and emotions of the dead, all the lingering presence of the mourners that come here, day after day; they stare back at Dom through those eyes.

Dom nearly sinks to his knees, and masks it as a squat. Again, he turns to the plaque, and reads the epitaph:

Is beloved and will be sadly missed. Is lived on by two beautiful children.

It's a contradiction, sending her off and at the same time chaining her to Ian, and even to her stepdaughter Mya. Is Jean here or in some place beyond? The answer given underneath those possibilities, whether she's here or there, is that she's at least somewhere.

'Jean, I'm going to start living again, I'm going to bring our family back together.'

'Promise her.'

'Yes.'

Neil huffs. 'Say it.'

'I promise, Jean.'

'Speaking it aloud takes it away from doubt,' says Neil, down beside him now, the prosthetic hand against the plaque again, caressing it like a child's cheek. 'She knows you've promised now.'

Dom could shout, or cry, or collapse to the ground. He feels capable of all of it in the same breath. They all clash in his mind, and he feels something in his temple swell, and then he feels nothing again. Dom stays on his knees for a while, regaining his equilibrium. 'So what do I do now?' he whispers in conspiracy.

'Maybe,' says Neil softly, 'we can start by talking about it on the show tonight. But, for now, I think we should grab some lunch. What are your thoughts?'

'My thoughts are, a sandwich would be nice.'

Neil picks him up and leads him away, across the massive plain of green grass and arranged stone, until they pass the gates and Dom feels like he's just returned from an alien world to find himself in familiar territory.

'You're looking even more tense than usual,' says

Neil.

'I'm just thinking,' replies Dom.

'She would want you to revisit, if you forgot to say something.'

'I forgot to say that I'm sorry.'

'For letting her go?'

'For killing her.'

Neil nods as if in a classroom. 'Interesting.'

'And 'interesting' is all you have to say? We're not talking about the fucking weather here, Neil. We can't all live in your fucking fantasy world.'

Neil's face bears the barb, and hardens. 'Did you kill her with a gun?'

'No.'

'A knife?'

'No.'

'Poison?'

'Shut up.'

'Maybe a pillow on the face?'

'Shut up!'

'Oh, I got it! Maybe she's not actually in that grave, she's lying on the bottom of the Yarra River in—'

Just like that, without thought or intent, Dom's hand is gripping Neil's neck. The false hand caresses Dom's forearm in a loving gesture, and the eyes are warm. Dom is shaking. He doesn't know which way to turn things, whether he wants to hurt Neil or not. His mind is wild, all his pure straight-minded thoughts slipping away and evaporating under a growing flame.

'Grip tighter, Dom.'

Dom complies. It strikes him that he might have only done it because Neil told him to.

'Tighter, even. Make me gasp for breath and beg for mercy.' His voice is strong, as if Dom's grip is barely tighter than the average shirt collar. 'It's funny, isn't it? I bet you don't lose your temper like this very often, except when no one is watching. I bet you just love feeling the energy of it. Do you feel something, Dom?'

'… Yes.'

'What is it?' asks Neil with an impish grin.

'Anger.'

'No. It's not anger, is it?'

'It's sin.'

'Ah. An interesting word. You can let go of me now.'

Dom complies. 'Do you appraise everyone like an Antiques Roadshow piece?'

'Only the ones that catch my eye,' says Neil. 'Well. I've decided that tonight, we're going to talk about sin.'

235

Community radio tends to lend itself to cramped studios; Dom is in the guest seat, facing Neil, who's surrounded by faders and controls and second-hand computer screens. One of Dom's arms is against the back of the CD player, and the other is close to being tangled in the venetian blind. Neil rocks forward, one hand sliding across the faders:

'Welcome back, this is Night Hymn on 3EZ Radio. I'm experimenting with a new segment here, a little bit of mixing it up and giving the audience, and myself, a new perspective and a change from hearing the same voice prattle on the way I do. I'm introducing, for the first and possibly last time, Dom's Decree.'

Silence is not golden in radio. Dom clears his throat, the sound grumbling down into the ether of radio waves, and decides that he's being ridiculous; it isn't this hard to talk. Then again, it's only been half a minute since a mic and pair of headphones were thrust at him without explanation.

'I guess I would have prepared a subject, but Neil isn't much for telling the hosts of new segments about their sudden starring role much in advance.'

Neil's tiny giggle sneaks onto the airwaves.

'I've had an interesting day,' says Dom. He's speaking to no one, not even Neil. The revelation emboldens him. 'I went to visit my wife's grave. Jean died about nine months ago, and her last years were always about the seizures. We have a son who was barely two at the time, and he was adding to the strain. Mya, my daughter from my first marriage, was home at that time too, but … well, she was barely home enough to be helpful, I guess.'

He looks away before continuing, not even speaking directly into the mic:

'I got frustrated, a lot. None of the meds they kept giving her were working, and the best ones were giving her side-effects just as bad. I'm the one who told her, "Go and get the elective surgery, let them operate". Jean didn't want it. "No quacks are going to tinker with my brain", she said. And I pushed. And she said yes. She said it was because she loved me enough to trust me.'

Dom expects Neil to butt in here, ask the questions about to be answered anyway, pervade the airwaves with his uncanny influence. Dom and Neil catch each other's eyes, and the look silences Dom. Neil has his hands drawn up, supporting his head, covering his mouth. The eyes stare forward like searchlights, drifting now and again.

'She died on the operating table.'

Neil is still silent. The eyes still wander. If it were anyone else, Dom would be infuriated that he was seemingly paying no attention.

'And if everyone has a sin to bear, I think that's mine.'

'That you let her die or that you sent her to the place of her death?' Neil's intrusion is without the usual melodious tone. The words are rough and unplanned.

'What's the difference? They both feel the same to me.'

'She died out of devotion to you. She died because she loved you enough to trust you. I think that's a very noble death. I think it has beauty.'

Another silence. The large clock ticks three times, and in that, there are nine new flashes on the phone. It's said the radio station was forced into supplying a multi-line phone just for Neil's show. Neil allows himself a slight smile, staring at the phone without moving to answer any of the calls, and Dom can only perceive that he has marked Dom's Decree as a radio success.

'You don't really care, do you?'

'Hm?' Neil is not taken aback, not shocked; there are no mortified gasps. Just another form of 'interesting'.

'I'm dragged onto radio and I say something that has haunted me for the better part of a year. And you're just smiling at the phone.'

'I think you're putting it in a negative light.' The

old melody is back, the smooth words that flicker in the air and slip through the chink in anyone's armour.

'I think I'm saying it as anyone would see it.'

'Hm?' Neil clicks on the line, switches off his mic, and answers the first caller with the sing-song of a receptionist. He's doing it again. He knows just how to get Dom to display real emotion.

Neil's mic comes alive again. 'And we have our first caller for Dom's Decree, the inaugural Jerome from Brighton. I'm always surprised to hear our broadcast gets as far as the affluent east, you know.'

'Yeah, we get it.' The voice is blank, searching for substance in the ether. 'Dom, I know the feeling.'

'Hm?' This time the filler is from Dom.

'My sister wanted to go bungee-jumping ... it was probably about three years ago, and I told her to get over it and do it, she was all scared and what if this happens, that happens, you know? Well, this and that happened, and, yeah, that's my sin. It's a word I haven't used before, but that's kind of what it feels like.'

The next ten minutes are punctuated with disaster and 'sin', of an endless role of callers, all running through Neil as the puppet master, bringing their own stories and their own reasons for guilt beyond logical explanation. None of them are directly to blame; they did not nail the lid onto the coffin, but they all stand

239

over it as the villain, the final mover of the person's chain of causality. They all claim to have carried the scissors that cut the thread of fate.

Dom can only blink and remember to breathe. And in front of him, there's Neil, sitting in a squeaking throne; his smile is of omniscience, as if it were all planned, as if he really were the puppet master of it all. Neil giveth, and Neil taketh away.

And in a second, Dom sees it; the cravings of Neil Loewenberg. The way he stares at the phones as the people flood in with their voices, their minds. Neil peruses minds, he seeks sources of contact and mingling. For Neil, the experience of life is one shared universally, the joy and the tragedy of living played out in front of an attentive audience.

More voices call out through the ether of radio. And, just like at the graveyard, the strange predatory creature named Neil Loewenberg accounts for them and incorporates them into himself.

Neil the hungry predator looks at Dom the rabbit. The fathomless eyes seem to say 'I will save you'.

Neil never accepts a ride from Dom; there's a train station ten minutes walk from the site of the radio station (a spare portable in a university – nothing but the best) but unless they're having a drink somewhere afterwards, he insists on the walk.

'Get in the car,' says Dom.

'Thanks, but no need.'

'Neil,' he says with a balanced voice, 'please just get in the car.'

'Nope.' Neil smiles. He has the intuition of a child about to be scolded. 'You don't see too happy that Dom's Decree was such a success.'

'Success!' Dom's voice is everywhere in that carpark, it's like the world is shouting with him. 'Success! How can anything with that kind of misery be considered a success?'

Neil laughs, loud and uproariously. Before Dom knows it, they're nose-to-nose. 'Bullshit. You enjoyed hearing it all. Like a moth to the flame, Dom. '

'I'm not like you.'

'Collective consciousness suggests otherwise.'

'What?'

'See, you're stuck in that little zone where you treat people too separately from each other. There's three levels, right, and us as individuals are at the middle level. Underneath is our bodies and biology, where we're all the same, and above is our minds and our consciousness, where we're all the same.' Neil grabs Dom's shirt like he's about to instigate a mugging. 'Get out of the middle zone, Dom, and open your mind a little beyond a couple of individuals who are no different from you. Open up to the whole experience. Embrace it.'

Dom's mouth works, almost chewing, as he tries to take all this in. Neil's talking faster, more frantically, and Dom wonders how much of this is premeditated and how much of it is just the words of some hidden demon, some generated complex that responds in reflex.

'Being an individual is lovely, but lonely, Dom. Don't you agree?'

'Whatever you say, Neil.'

Dom sits on the bonnet of his car, looking at Neil afresh. His youth, or at least his youth in relation to Dom. His wooden hand. His spotlight-eyes. For the first time, Dom wonders who Neil mourns.

'I'll get in the car,' Neil says abruptly.

Dom lies in bed, feeling like he's drowning in scotch, congratulating himself on getting through the day. He's tumbling his mobile, switched off, from one hand to the other. Neil was never apologetic for his barbs, and only pushed harder when Dom showed resistance. There were no warm goodbyes when Neil was dropped off at the station. Dom tried to drink away his anger, and ended up throwing his glass against the wall anyway. The sound of smashing glass was about the only thing that could break his focus on his own temper.

Ian is still not asleep either, although he's locked into his cot. His eyes peep over at Dom, watching him, waiting for anything that might be funny, or a cue that they're going to rush out to the lounge room again and pick up the TV remote. Kids live in constant expectation; it would be cute if it didn't grate on the adult's patience so much.

He can't sleep, so he switches on his mobile again. It lights up and screeches; missed message, missed message, missed voice message, missed call, missed Neil, again and again. He decides to only pay the voice message any regard; no greeting, no formality, just the second half of a conversation with its beginnings in Neil's mind:

'I want Dom's Decree back for next Sunday. If you can pop in for any of the other shows you're more than welcome as well, I don't have any guests for you to compete with. I really enjoy our one-on-ones, Dom, I think we can really learn a lot from each other. The gloss of the fresh friendship is falling away and we're really getting to know each other. And with the way things are, I think we can forge something real strong here.

'I have things cooking in my skull. It's all good stuff. I want to save you, Dom, and I think that maybe you can save me a little as well. God's will, and all that. I'm serious, Dom. This is the last point where you can exit. After this is the odyssey. I'm not kidding. I'm real excited. If I get no call by midnight, then we can really get down to business.'

Dom checks his watch. It's ten minutes past midnight.

The next morning does not bring a headache in the same way that Dom is used to. There is instead a total blasting of the senses, a numbness beyond headache, until he gets up and regrets being alive. The rest of the scotch goes down the sink. This is the turning point for his old habits. It has to be. Alcoholism is a death wish in slow motion, and so many are trying to teach him to live and drop the harmful stuff that, for once, it feels easier to flow with them.

A wail slices through his head as if his brain were wrapped in barbed wire and he gains the urge to so something, anything, to make the kid happy and send him on his way to the babysitter. Work today. Or, at least, his job today. The only work is keeping in the job.

Then a remarkable thought pops into his barbed-wire brain. Fuck it. Simple as that. The phone picks itself up, dials itself, and his mouth, fuzzy and dry, mouths something similar to 'fuck it' and 'I quit'. Ian gurgles with every curse, his sign of approval. Dom hangs up, leaving that old rouge-affected cow Marge to fume to herself for the rest of the day over the rudeness of some people.

He dials again; the numbers fly past, easily and in a steady rhythm. Dom could have last dialled the number yesterday. He's not sure how many months it has actually been.

'Rob Traminer here.'

'Rob, it's Dom Milford.'

A pause. Then, a small laughter disguised in a long sigh. 'Dom-in-ic! Holy shit.' Another pause. 'Holy shit. I got around to thinking you'd just dropped off the face of the earth.

'Not too far off that,' says Dom

'So … how's things?'

'Better. I was wondering if I could pick up the pieces a little if you know what I mean.'

'I do, and I was worried you'd get to that.'

Dom can see the kiln-dried face of Rob Traminer, set in its fault lines and sun scars, aged before its time by too many cheap solariums. Rob does business like a piranha strips away a cow carcass, with a face like a golem's. Great poker face. The boys at the firm would

245

all gather for cards, every week, and although Dom loved the games, he hated the inevitability of his losses.

'The thing is, Dom, I obviously had to fill all the positions that you could possibly come back to if you were considering coming back. Of course I kept things open as long as possible, and we were going fine for a bit, but the young kid we have now has been here for six months and it'll be my arse on the frying pan if I try to sack him now.'

'That makes sense.'

'Dom, I can get you a little marketing gig, but it wouldn't be much better than phone sales or book-keeping. A rung or two down, so to speak.'

'Okay.'

'I'm guessing you're good for it? I've done my best here, Dom.'

'Fuck your best.' Oh God that felt good!

'Eh?'

'I lost my wife, Rob. Of course I needed more than a month or two. Fine that you can't keep exactly the same job open for me, I understand that, but going back to being a corporate whipping boy? Under your 'young kid' who is probably half my age? I say again, fuck your best.'

'This is business, Dom, and if you can't hack a reshuffle then I've got no olive branch for you.'

'God forbid I take any hand-me-downs from you,' says Dom, hanging up. He feels so calm. The heart is erratic, but the head is placid through the pangs of hangover. Ian rolls around on the floor, entertaining himself. Dom watches his son for a while, then the phone rings in his hand. It digs deep into his ears, and he groans aloud, a sound Ian copies. It's already a busy day for someone freshly unemployed.

'Hello?'

'Oh, Dom, hi, it's Alice. I was just a little worried and all, with Ian not here yet …'

'I'm not at work today, so I was thinking I'd spend a little time with him for once.'

'I'd say that's nice,' says Alice, her voice dropping an octave, 'except I'm now going to ask what's going on instead.'

'You're not being clear.' There's an impulse to swear, find some fault or sin in her, but this is Alice and some bridges can't afford to be burned. Good babysitters are hard to come by.

'Will you be going to work tomorrow, Dom?'

'What kind of question is that?'

'Will you?'

'No.' Dom stifles a sigh; are women always this perceptive? Jean used to frighten him like this; it was as if she were psychic.

'So what's happened?'

'I quit.'

'Dom!'

'So it means it might be a little longer before I get you the money that I owe, I'm sorry. I'll send you to the Gold Coast for a month, or something like that.'

Alice rumbles, magma bubbling up somewhere in her body. It seethes away, and Dom waits until she has the composure to talk again, sounding incredibly tired. 'What's gotten into you, Dom? Are you going back to that old job of yours then? You said it reminded you of too much.'

'I kind of shut that door as well. I had an altercation with the old boss.'

'Right.'

'But it won't be too hard for me to find something.'

'Of course.'

'Then I'll send you to Queensland on a gravy train for your troubles.'

'I'll look forward to it.'

'Any other notes in that instrument, or is it all the one note?'

'Don't push it, Dom.'

Ian yelps. He's stepped on something. Ian hops, steps back on the foot, and yelps again, falling over in a shriek that follows him down.

'I've got to go, Alice.'

'What did he do?'

'Bye, Alice.'

'Wait, Do—'

Ian picks himself up, tries to walk towards Dom while screaming in an unholy racket, and loses balance, falling a second time. The tiles show the trail, a red polka-dot pattern. Dom grabs the foot and peers into a pulsing gape, with a sparkle somewhere within. It turns out to be a slither of broken glass. Is that from last night, when the glass smashed against the wall? The stain is still there, so some bones of the broken skeleton must have lingered around after the cleanup as well. Ian's attempt to stand on the foot again has driven the glass completely in.

'Stay still.'

Dom rushes to the bathroom, the hands slapping away anything in the drawers and medicine cabinet that isn't a pair of tweezers; finally finding the tweezers, he heads back into the kitchen, punctuated by the rises and falls of Ian's more and more fervent screaming. He's entered a blind panic, not understanding why his foot hurts and why he can't stand up. He's so proud of standing and running.

The foot's so small, tweezers are not much of an option. Dom, still riding a wave of self-assurance that allowed him to tell two people to fuck off in the same morning, dives in for the glass shard nonetheless. It's small but thick, and blood is surging out as the body tries to pump the foreign body out. Ian kicks, yells, knocks his head on the kitchen tiles again and again, raging like a madman about to get the sedative. Dom's head throbs and he gets impatient, making one last attempt for the glass, and he swears he can feel the flesh straining against the invasion.

'Okay then …'

Ian is writhing, wanting his father to let go, snap his fingers and rewind the whole scene to when the foot was intact and working without agony. Dom instead wraps the foot lightly in a cloth, wraps another cloth tighter around the ankle to do something about all that blood flow, bundles Ian in his arms like a damsel in distress and surges out of the driveway with his Peugeot. He knows he's saying assuring things to his son – 'relax, it's all good, it's all okay, just a quick car trip and you can count the trees if you want …' – but the white noise of his words is drowned out by Ian's insistent wails.

Dom drives with no attention to the road, only one hand on the wheel, the other trying to keep Ian in one spot. The cloth is too loose around his foot to soak up anything, and the old stains of apple juice are overtaken with red.

Ian's sanity is loose and out of Dom's hands. The throat must be sore and unwilling to endure any more screaming by now, but Ian still vomits out a wail or two, although with less force. Dom glances at the foot when he can, avoiding cars in a blaring of beeps and profanities, and feels his own sanity throbbing and wanting to collapse.

Finally, the hospital. It has a name, he's used and remembered it plenty of times. Who cares? Ian is bundled up and rushed in, and damn all those car crash victims and haemorrhage sufferers, damn all those drug overdoses and young partiers on the wrong side of a serrated knife, they can all wait, Ian is going to ICU where the doctors and surgeons will consult their spellbook-clipboards and wave their magic wand-scalpel and make Ian all better. Goddamn it, they owe him.

Reception doesn't need to be yelled at to put aside a bed, like it always happens in desperate movies; the thin young woman, pale from fluorescent light, sees a toddler bleeding and cites an alarm in stoic tones, eyes saying 'poor baby, help him, help him' and Dom's eyes saying 'yes, yes, help him'.

A more sober doctor pokes his cold gaze into the wound, looking dry and sinewy despite the continuing flow of blood. 'Yes, we'll have to remove the glass and bind this as best we can.'

'So stitches then?'

'Well, I wouldn't say so on a foot this size—'

'Look at the size of it! What are you going to do, put a bloody band-aid on it?'

'I won't recommend stitches. We'll just have to clean and wrap it and let the skin reseal itself.'

Dom blinks, breaths; his mind catches up with him, a precious thing left behind somewhere during the drive.

'Sorry. So will he be here overnight?'

'It's still morning, so I doubt it. We'll see what we can do to help him with his stress, and it'll all depend on how he goes after we remove the glass. We should be able to get started on it fairly soon.'

'I can be there for it, right?'

The doctor nods, eyes already vacant and lost in an inner world of anatomy and details. Dom briefly wonders what it would be like to be so impervious to the stress and anxiety of others.

Dom moves away, thinking about anything but the task at hand; he muses over how he'll have to clean those kitchen tiles more thoroughly, how he'll scrub and sweep them until he can pace every tile without hearing a chink or crunch.

This isn't fair. The last time he was at this point, with the stale smell of the hospital on him, he was bouncing between the waiting room and the fresh air at the doors, wanting nothing more than to walk away and forget it all, before he had steeled himself to find out the results of a brain surgery that, it turned out, ended in 'complications'.

A missed call on his mobile. He ignores it, hoping against hope that it isn't Neil with another proclamation. He remembers midnight. The fairy tale has either begun or ended, and Neil has placed himself as the storyteller, the one turning the page and deciding how the days would be different from each other. Is this Neil's world, where Dom tells a former boss to 'fuck his best' and sees his son's foot open up like a second mouth?

The bland mechanical voice tells him about the missed message, and it plays:

'Dom, tell me if Ian is okay. Then tell me if you're okay.'

Only when he's out front of the hospital, back turned to the sharp wind, does he call Alice and bring her up to speed.

'Ow, poor thing,' she says. 'How long will it take to heal?'

'Probably a while. It's going to bruise his pride

more than anything else, not being able to walk properly for a while.'

'True. Your little imp runs circles around me when he's top gear.'

There's a while where the conversation wanders, and talk is about the things that Ian does when waking or running. The emotion suggests that he'll never walk again, spending life as a little urchin with a crutch and blue eyes telling of suffering.

'Dom, this really has you shaken, doesn't it?'

'It's just not right to see him bleed like that. He nearly gave himself a concussion from head-butting the tiles.'

'Did you have someone to talk to like this when Jean was in the hospital?'

'Hey, only Neil is allowed to be that forward.'

'Neil?'

'Um, no I didn't, I mean.' To Dom, Neil needs no explanation. He is Dom's enigma and no one else's.

Night Hymn comes along on Wednesday night. Dom, exhausted from two days of trying to convince Ian that the wrapping around his foot shouldn't be picked at, is adamant he will not be doing Dom's Decree; he just sits and listens.

Emma's sobs are swallowed and sucked in, but the

sound of them is still carrying across the ether. Neil's face is passive. His voice, however, could have the backing of a grand piano behind it. Dom still can't shake himself from the spell, the majesty of Neil's tones.

'Now Emma, I want you to listen to me. I can't talk to you in the capacity of a counsellor or a therapist, obviously. And I'm guessing you want me to say something about God here, obviously. Am I right in saying you want me to tell you that God is there for you, and will heal your wounds?'

A sniff.

'I can't say it in those words.'

'But ...'

'Hang on, I've got a sucker punch coming and it's a good one.'

There's a little noise that sounds halfway between a sniffle and a giggle.

'We are people. Right? We are people with our own intentions, our own purposes. I don't believe much in predestination or being bound to a destiny that affects our daily lives. We make our lives. We have power over our physical lives. And we have the power to heal ourselves.

'All people, I think, are equal. We are children of God. But God does not coddle us. When a child falls, scrapes his knee, cries a little and winces at the pain, will God be there to kiss the wound and make it better, and put a bandaid over it?'

Dom finds himself thinking about Ian, safe and sound back home with a saintly Alice watching over him.

'Even God can't make it go away, just like that. You need to not forget your equals. You need to not forget your friends, and you need to not forget your family, because you can bet that they haven't forgotten about you. And I'll tell you to not forget about God too, because even though he can't send His blessing down in a beam of light and take away all your worries, but I'm hoping that keeping Him in mind will warm your heart and make things easier.'

Emma says something, lost to her own sniffling— Dom can't even remember why she's so upset. He hasn't really been listening. There are so many callers, so many guests, that the faceless names are easy to forget.

Emma is sent away, the shepherd dismissing his sheep back to the meadow at the bottom of the hill. 'Okay all, I've run a little overtime, which is a no-no as far as this station is concerned, even if we're just flicking to a satellite feed. So, a fare-thee-well, a song and then some waffle from Germany for God knows how long. Peace, and hope to have your attention again next time.' The red light goes off and a song goes on.

'What's this one?' asks Dom.

'Radiohead. Haunting and beautiful. Never try to contradict a mood, Dom, it always makes things worse. You've got to ride emotions like a rollercoaster.'

'Yes, you've said that to me plenty of times. You said my grieving period was just one big dip.'

'And you're climbing back up. Exactly. So have you fucked Alice yet?'

Dom sighs. 'Funny that you're the one always turning his nose up at bad language on the radio.'

'That's radio. Even community radio can be a tad civil.' Neil winks, the mischief of an urchin written across his face. 'Besides, you know I love riling you up.'

'Take pity on an old man.'

'In your forties and you write yourself off like that? And you expect me to take you seriously, Dom, I'm not sure if that's an effective policy, you know? You're the old bumbler in a comedy flick.'

'So says the twenty-something whippersnapper.'

Neil grins widely, all teasing and chosen words aside. Dom squirms, thinking that he can only imagine the thoughts that run through his friend's mind; what are the pure thoughts of someone who seems to think of himself as a prophet?

The song ends, and Neil flicks on the satellite feed to the news in German. He shrugs dramatically and ushers Dom out the studio, and follows behind all the way to the carpark with a private smile. They get into the car, and Dom drives off with Neil in tow.

'Go left here.'

'Towards the city? Why?'

'We need a night to open up. We need an odyssey, and sometimes being on your feet in heathen lands helps the effect a little. Trust me.'

Dom complies, following the dark road towards the inner suburbs of the city in a heavy silence. Dom thinks for a moment whether he should call Alice and tell her that he'll be late to relieve her of Ian, but the thought washes away as Neil prods him into turning onto this road, then that, and finally Dom slips his car into a small lot on the northern end of Melbourne's CBD. From here, Neil walks, with Dom tripping on his heels. Neil has still said nothing about where they're going. They turn left, then right, seemingly in random movements until the litany of street names—Arden, Queensberry, a quick jaunt along Franklin, and back again via the northern reaches of Elizabeth, circling the old and new, the kitsch and the conservative, all in one fell swoop—lose meaning and it just becomes left, right, across this road, along that tram dinging along.

'What am I looking for, Neil?'

'I'm not going to tell you. Watch the people's faces. Read the graffiti. Get a feel for it all. Like I am.'

Sure enough, Neil looks fit to burst. His prosthetic hand runs along a small line of marked text—'God is dead'—along the rear wall of a pub. The philosophy of angry youth rushes past, and Dom learns that the police are puppets, that force is the weapon of the weak, that rainbows are fucking stupid. Every letter is sprayed on in frenzied lines, wedged between unknown signatures, every gesture of drawing a mark of determined need. These people want to be known, they want their thoughts to be known. They are singular and lonely, and have the need to spew things out.

'Are these people like you, then?'

'Ah, I think you're starting to get it.'

'There's a world of difference. All this is so angry.'

'Not all of it is. We've come across an unfortunate wall. There's satire and there's beauty too if you're lucky. And there's passion. That's the lesson.'

They move forward, faster, faster, and the graffiti fades away as lights start to flicker above them.

Brunswick Street opens up. They move along, and figures slip past, some averting their eyes and others making a point of meeting the eyes of every passerby;

bookshops and apartment blocks stare at each other from across the road, and cars and trams cruising along in the middle of it all. A plain-looking dining hall looms up in the distance, the devil-eyed Cupid of the Little Creatures brand watching over it all, and crowds flow in and out for a badly-cooked bowl of chips and a beer to wash it all down.

'Is this something to do with Australian nightlife? Culture? That dining hall sums it up.'

'It does and it doesn't. Stick around in that hall and you'll see some beautiful things.'

'Neil—'

'Sh. You talk too much. Far too much. Just let the mouth close and let everything else wash over, we're in the twilight of things, and night becomes day, and day becomes night, I swear it's all at once…'

'It's already night, Neil—'

'I said sh.'

They head up Brunswick, then turn back. Neil has something else on his mind, and Dom can't help but think that the so-called lessons are made up, a way of killing time, a way of making something out of nothing. He still feels invigorated; the walking of the past hour has been the most he has done for some time, and he doesn't feel tired. Neil is talking to himself in a mumble.

'Over here,' he says abruptly. 'I want to get a quick drink and chill out. I want a calm before I storm.'

Neil slides into a pub with the professionalism of a regular drinker. Dom follows, orders a scotch when Neil already has his beer, an English-looking ale.

'You don't have a plan at all, do you?'

'Do you?'

Dom laughs as an answer, and regrets the mockery. Neil does not even listen. His eyes flicker, and show no anger, only the same raw energy.

'I don't need a plan. I have a destination. I have a goal. And I think you have the same goal as me.'

'And you said that something in me intrigued you. You said you wanted to save me and that I might be able to save you a little too.'

'You have a good memory.'

'You barely remember a thing you talk about, do you?'

The eyes fix on Dom, and he realises how wrong he is. Neil, forget something? The expression on Dom's face right now will be etched somewhere deep in Neil's mind for longer than life. For a second, he thinks he can see his own face, through the eyes now staring at him.

Neil looks so gaunt now, stretched thin, exhausted from his own emotions. With the tiny streak under his eyes, and the way his posture is beginning to curl, the classic armadillo pose of the relaxed-yet-guarded, he almost looks human for once. He gulps his beer, and droops as if deflated.

'Neil, are you okay?'

'Beer takes away the edge a bit. I like that sometimes.'

'But the way you talk, it's as if you want my emotions to be as high as possible.'

'Yup.'

'Then—'

'Dom, I keep saying you talk too much. Sh. Let me mellow, I'd like to have a little calm before the storm.'

Neil takes his ale to the street window, watches the people and cars and trams pass by, and no light reflects on him so that he looks like a thin shadow, wavering except for that hand that will never move, and to Dom it seems that Neil is about to fade away, but he can see the smile, the wicked little grin playing across the cheeks. Instead of crying out to his companion to keep himself together, stop, explain why he's suddenly so morose, Dom instead wonders at the limits of Neil's emotional range; and, in the angles of darkness and the ordered symphony of traffic that moves before him, how even a morose man can strike such a beautiful image.

Neil drains his ale. 'We go now, Dom.'

They go.

The night of Melbourne seems vast, and the streets stretch for forever, but Neil knows exactly where he's going. They stop into an underground café, small ceilings and cozy spaces, circled around a jazz act which croons along with the condescending head-bobbing of the clientele, and they sit and 'mellow on good terms', in Neil's words. And Dom is only starting to catch onto the tunes, and weave along with the notes in the air when Neil drags him out, proclaiming their time there over, and they are on the trams giggling to themselves like drunks. Dom can't explain where his lightness of spirit has come from. They stop at a place that's still the north of Melbourne, although Dom can't say where they've gone and what route they've taken, while Neil guides him to a corner spot where the dagger-sharp tones of urban rock hit up against the inner walls, like prisoners clambering to get out and dash through the night. Dom enters, and the lead guitarist is in his own trace, perfectly visible from the front door. A harmonica is strung around his collar with a thin steel brace, and he sings between bursts of harmonica notes, a one-man band backed up by others who may or may not share his vision, but they at least have their own communal spirit. Dom sees them from afar, then is dragged up close, only mildly aware of the admission fee Neil plucks from him, only barely feeling the press of shoulders and seeing the collection of like-minded grins. Neil turns to him and smiles a grin above them all, and with his height he rises above the rabble.

There's a tiny glimmer in the back of Dom's mind, a temporary moment where he swears that, for a moment, he can almost see Neil on equal terms, and might even have the same look in his eyes. And the moment is gone, and he is just Dom again, and he forgets the sense of multiplicity that threatened to remind him that he is only barely an individual, that his boundaries are so thin. It times itself with the music, which rises, falls, and plays with boundaries, teasing the framework of reality in a way that drugs are supposed to do.

He watches Neil, moving in a wild refrain, eyes staring at the visage of the divine, somewhere beyond everything within Dom's comprehension. Neil equates God with passion, and salvation to rapture. He imagines all the things that Neil must be seeing, and the way that he already has the power to dissect souls; an appraising young man who can take to flaws and sins, sensitivities in the wild working movement of humans and their minds, and apply his own spiritual psychology to it like a balm. He imagines that Neil can see colours beyond the scope of eyeballs, and must be sweating so profusely under that shirt, dreaming of lands where people are passionate and enamoured with their own lives, and by extension the lives of others, a place where music like this chimes forever, leaving quiet hymns to shame, and fishing the spirit out of the body to take a soft little gander at the Gnostic nature of all things.

The song ends, and the walls are solid again.

Neil sneaks up and whispers in Dom's ear; 'And you know what? I don't think they're even that good.'

Dom drives back; Neil is practically speaking in tongues. 'I just want people to understand ... you know, the way the mind works ... we're all so damn sensitive and we burn ourselves out ... I think every man's mind is God, well, women too, I'm not sexist ... I'm trying to tell you, Dom, listen, I think I'm onto something here ...'

Dom pulls up aside Neil's small home, practically a cottage, probably a parting gift from deceased parents.

'We could talk about it on the show ... you and me, you know? ... the way the band was playing, they were no good, but it was all the same thing, everything I'm going for ... music isn't the only way, but it's the easiest way ... I can do it, you know, without tunes, I did it once, it was like a trance or something ...'

Dom opens the passenger door. Neil stumbles out, limbs weighed down with spirit as heavy as a dosage of alcohol.

'I want you to understand me, Dom, really, I think you could get there as well, and the way you looked at me in the bar, wow! You know? We can see each other now, you can see me for what I am and I can see you for what could be, and it's exciting … look, look, Dom, my hand is shaking, ha hah …'

Dom guides Neil to his front door. Neil's feet are reluctant, wanting to plant themselves in the ground, strike a balance, form a podium out of a slab of pavement. They find their way to Neil's door, bit by bit.

'Now see here, Dom, and I say "see here" like a shameless old man, I want to really speak to you now, I want to really bring you in, and tell you things, and share so many of my thoughts with you, because I need someone to share them with, someone who really gets it and knows the thrill, and I can tell you so many things, really, I could even tell you how I lost my hand, it was when I was a kid and I was at the zoo and …'

The story never finishes. Dom walks back to his car, and it's not until he's in the driver's seat that he realises Neil followed him back, like a pet. The comparison is sickening to Dom. Their eyes meet, and Dom is afraid and somehow disgusted. He doesn't know what to do. He doesn't know what Neil wants. Now that he thinks of it, despite all his declarations and intentions, he doesn't know what Neil really wants. Which moment is the one with clarity? The emotional high of the music and the feeling of minds touching in the emptiness, or this moment here, where he looks at Neil as himself, as Dom Milford, and feels the hair on the back of his neck stand on end?

He still doesn't know what to do. So he eases the car door shut with Neil outside.

Neil's eyes burn with betrayal, the glass only barely a barrier. 'What the fuck is this, Dom? I open up and you close down? I'm searching for God and you abandon me when I need a companion? I'm giving you something to care about!' His right eye twitches. 'I'm saving you from yourself, from being a lonely man! You pathetic sack of shit!'

Dom starts the car and Neil thumps on the glass with his prosthetic hand. Dom drives off and Neil chases him for a while, pumping his arms like a track runner in the middle of the road, until the car turns a corner, and suddenly things seem all too quiet.

Dom gets home, and staggers to the front door as if drunk; his head is spinning, and he can't work out where the night has ended, can't even work out the state of his own mind. He moves from room to room, and everything is neat and ordered, a sure sign of Alice, and he finally finds her in the bedroom, curled up on top of his bed. Ian is in his cot, spread-eagled with legs bunched up in a strange sign of modesty. He's been picking at the bandaging around his foot again.

Dom takes no time to appreciate the scene. He shakes Alice awake. 'Mmmwhaa, hmm? Five more minutes …'

'Alice.'

'Oh, Dom. Sorry if I don't get out the homecoming trumpets.'

'Sorry I'm so late.'

'Not as sorry as you will be for interrupting my sleep. Nick off.'

'You're in my bed.'

Alice's head is buried in a pillow, so any smirk is unseen. She pats the mattress. 'It's a queen bed, smoothie, there's room.'

'But how much would I owe for you looking after—'

A growl; Dom stops. Alice reaches out absently with one hand, It eventually wraps around one of Dom's hands. 'And you tell me off for playing the same tone in a conversation all the time.'

'What?'

'If I wanted pay, you moron, I would have called

you up on that so-called debt ages ago. Let it go.'

'But you—'

'Or write it off as charity, I don't care.'

'But—'

'And if you say 'but' one more time I will hurt you and make it look like an accident. Sleep. I want sleep. He was loud tonight.'

Her hand retreats as she squirms deeper into the covers and hugs herself. Dom plays the pragmatist, wondering about all his options, and the only thing that solidifies his decision to move away and set up his makeshift bed on the couch is the presence of Ian. He's always been a light sleeper, and a wounded foot has made him even more restless lately.

He works himself into the couch, digging into the cushions and upholstery the same way Alice has taken root in his bed, when it finally occurs to him that there was a photo album brushing up against her back, occupying the other space on the bed. He saw it as soon as he had walked in; in fact, he had perceived and interpreted it before he had picked apart that the human-shaped figure next to it was Alice. For a second, he imagined Alice and Ian leafing through the album. Or did Alice discover it after Ian had collapsed in a fit of protest and overwhelming fatigue?

He starts to sleep, and forgets about the album by

the time he drifts off. By the time he wakes up, Alice is relatively groomed and the album is back in its proper place on the shelf. She sits at the kitchen table, smiling in that way that seems indecisive, as if she can't work out why she's smiling. Dom smiles back.

The phone rings. Mornings are becoming regularly crowded with phone calls. Dom sighs and picks up. 'Hello?'

'Hello, I'm speaking to Dom Milford?'

'You are.'

'You're listed as an emergency contact for Neil Loewenberg.'

'Am I?' A pause. 'What's happened to him?'

'He was hit by a car last night. He's here in a coma.'

Aside from some gravel marks on his face, Neil's face looks peaceful. The rest of him, however, is covered in wrappings and tubes. The prosthetic hand has been partially removed, so that there's only a scratched-up stump with a slot.

Dom relaxes himself. Neil's not there anymore. For now, at least. Neil Loewenberg became a madman or a prophet, where the two can be distinguished, and when he spoke on the airwaves he corrupted everyone in earshot with an unbearable yearning for thrill and happiness, for acceptance, and for cohesiveness, and for a dozen other ideals that probably contradicted themselves at some point or another.

Dom shakes his head. The spell of Neil feels confused now, and he finds himself wondering just how much of his own life Neil would have consumed. Would there have been a totality behind the individuals? Probably not for Neil. Despite his yearning, Neil would always have been a lonely individual, too wilful to surrender himself completely. Instead, Dom had surrendered himself to Neil, and completely forgotten about Jean. A refreshing jaunt, but somehow wrong to Dom, especially when Ian should be a constant reminder. And Mya, too. If Dom ever gets around to calling her. She probably would have liked Neil.

'Can you hear me, Neil?'

No response, from Neil or the machines.

'Thank you. You failed, but thank you. Somehow that makes it feel like a good thing anyway.'

Dom fancies he can hear, from somewhere in his own skull, the amused and derisive response from Neil.

A PROJECT OF

THE AUSTRALIAN LITERATURE REVIEW

The goal of The Australian Literature Review is to revitalise Australian fiction, to showcase vibrant and original Australian fiction, and to assist storytellers to further develop their fiction writing skills.

auslit.net

www.ingramcontent.com/pod-product-compliance
Lightning Source LLC
Chambersburg PA
CBHW070851250626
47159CB00003B/1031